The sound of ... approaching car made
the Mystery Kids turn their heads. A blue
car came along, and headed towards the
broken-down vehicle.

'Perhaps he'll stop to help,' said Holly.
'It can't be much fun breaking down
out here.'

As they watched, one of the men from
the stationary car stepped into the middle
of the road and waved his arms.

The moving car slowed and came to a
halt. The driver got out.

To the utter shock of the three friends,
two of the men threw themselves on the
driver and started dragging him towards
their own car. The driver of the first
car jumped back in and they heard the
motor roar.

There was a brief struggle as the two
men forced the driver of the second car
into the back.

'Oh, my gosh!' gasped Holly. 'They're
kidnapping him!'

# The Mystery Kids series

# THE MYSTERY KIDS

# Hostage!

## Fiona Kelly

**Hodder Children's Books**

a division of Hodder Headline plc

**Special thanks to Allan Frewin Jones**

Copyright © 1996 Ben M. Baglio
Created by Ben M. Baglio
London W6 0HE

First published in Great Britain in 1996
by Hodder Children's Books

The right of Fiona Kelly to be identified as
the Author of the Work has been asserted by
him in accordance with the Copyright, Designs
and Patents Act 1988.

10 9 8 7 6 5 4 3 2 1

A Catalogue record for this book is
available from the British Library

ISBN 0 340 65567 4

Typeset by Hewer Text Composition Services, Edinburgh
Printed and bound in Great Britain by
Cox & Wyman Ltd, Reading, Berks

Hodder Children's Books
a division of Hodder Headline plc
338 Euston Road
London NW1 3BH

# Contents

 # Kidnapped!

Holly Adams pulled herself along on her stomach through the prickly, spiny undergrowth. She paused and glanced back. Peter was right behind her, flat as a snake in the gorse. And directly behind him, Holly could see Miranda's round, saucer-eyed face staring straight at her through a tangle of heather.

Holly gave the special secret eyebrow-wiggle that meant, *Keep absolutely silent*. Her two companions nodded. Total silence was vital or the Mystery Kids' entire mission could fail.

Holly edged forwards and parted the screen of low brambles. Their quarry was about four metres away, facing away from them.

*At last*, thought Holly. They had been waiting for this moment for the past three days.

1

She made a tiny movement of her fingers towards Peter; the movement that meant, *Come forwards*.

Peter glided up alongside her.

Everything became perfectly still and quiet, as though the whole world was holding its breath.

'Oww!' Miranda yelled. 'Owwowwoww! I've got cramp!'

The bird was in the air in an instant, its wings cupping and unfolding as it sped low over the moorland and then soared high until it was just a black speck in the clear blue of the sky.

Peter sat up, his finger still poised on the button of his camera. He glared at Miranda, who was clutching her leg and howling. He was speechless with annoyance.

'Oh, Miranda!' exclaimed Holly.

'I'm in pain,' wailed Miranda, frantically massaging her foot.

Half a minute later her groans had subsided.

'Sorry about that,' she said, pulling her long blonde hair off her face. Her bright blue eyes turned to Peter. 'Did you manage to get a picture?'

'No,' said Peter, dryly.

'Oh, well,' Miranda grinned hopefully. 'You can't win 'em all, eh?'

'It was a merlin,' Peter said dully, as if he still couldn't quite believe what had happened. 'An adult male merlin. They're really rare these days. I've never seen one before.'

'Maybe we'll get another chance,' said Holly. 'We're here for another three days.'

'Take a picture of me instead,' said Miranda. 'The lesser spotted, blonde-haired Mystery Kid.' She gave Peter one of her widest, most cheerful grins.

'Twit!' said Peter with a laugh. He lifted the camera to his eye and took a quick snap of his friend.

Peter Hamilton, Miranda Hunt and Holly Adams were on a camping holiday on Trepolen Moor in the West Country.

It had been Mr Hamilton's idea. Peter's father had been sent on business to the area for a few days. The firm he worked for was setting up a large exhibition stand at the Royal West Country Show. It was during the school holidays, so Peter was to come along with him. There were only the two of them; Peter's mother had died when he was very young.

Peter and his father were making a camping holiday of it. But Mr Hamilton would be working most of the time, so it was agreed that Holly and Miranda could come along as well.

All that was needed was for the three friends to drag a second tent down out of the Hunts' attic and they were all set for an adventurous week on the moors!

And it had been fun, despite the changeable weather and one day of thick fog earlier in the week: they cooked on a portable gas stove; they roamed the bleak but beautiful moors with packed lunches and with Peter's camera always at the ready; and they zipped themselves up in sleeping-bags at night like bananas in their skins.

Then, on Thursday morning, they had finally caught sight of something special. *Falco columbarius*, Peter had read from his pocket book of British birds. A merlin!

And then Miranda had got cramp.

The three friends headed back to the campsite. There was a large packet of sausages waiting for them. Sausages, half a dozen free-range eggs and an enormous tin of beans. Lunch was going to be a real feast.

Peter shoved the sizzling sausages around in the frying pan while Miranda struggled with the tin of baked beans and a reluctant tin-opener.

'It's broken,' she said. She looked at Holly, who was deep in a fold-out tourist brochure. It had an annotated map on one side and details of local points of interest on the other. The Mystery Kids had picked the guide up the previous day in a little old grocer's shop in the nearby village.

'Holly, it's broken.'

'Of course it's not broken,' said Holly without even looking up. 'You're just useless with anything mechanical.'

Miranda snorted. 'I'm telling you this stupid thing is broken. D'you think I can't open a tin?'

Holly plucked tin and opener out of Miranda's hands.

'This is interesting,' Holly said as she opened the tin without even looking, the tourist guide spread out in her lap. 'There's

5

a place not all that far away called Dreath House.' She handed Miranda the open can. 'It's halfway across the moor, and it's open to the public.'

Miranda glared at the tin-opener then tipped the beans into a saucepan.

'What's there?' asked Peter. 'Anything interesting?'

' "Dreath House was formerly a coaching inn and a notorious smugglers' den," ' read Holly. ' "It has a restaurant and a museum of curiosities and is open from nine a.m. to nine p.m., seven days a week from May to October." ' Holly looked up, her grey eyes shining. 'Did you hear that?' she said. ' "A notorious smugglers' den." Does that sound good, or what?'

'Formerly,' said Miranda. 'It said "formerly". I expect it's just some tacky tourist trap now.'

'All the same,' said Peter, 'it should be worth a look. I wonder what a museum of curiosities is? It sounds dead mysterious.'

Holly grinned. 'And that's exactly what's been missing from this holiday so far: a good mystery for the Mystery Kids to solve!'

Holly loved mysteries. She had always loved mysteries, ever since she had first read *Harriet the Spy*. Harriet lived in New York and spent her time watching her neighbours and writing down all their activities and movements in a little notebook.

And then there was Holly's favourite television serial: *Spyglass*, in which her great hero, Special Agent John Raven, thwarted an endless succession of evil-doers.

But watching spy serials and reading books about mysterious goings-on just wasn't enough for Holly. Which is why she and Miranda set up their spying agency back home in Highgate, North London where they both lived. It was soon after this that they met up with Peter. They had quickly become friends, and together they managed to thwart a robbery at the very bank where Holly's mother worked!

The three of them even got mentioned in the newspapers: *MYSTERY KIDS FOIL BANK ROBBERY* proclaimed the headlines, which was how they came by their name. But that was quite a few mysteries ago. Holly Adams seemed to attract mysteries like a jam pot attracts wasps!

'So,' Holly said as she folded the brochure. 'Who's for a trip to Dreath House this afternoon?'

'Me!' Peter said, giving the plump brown sausages another turn in the pan before carefully cracking the eggs two at a time on the rim and pouring them into the fizzing oil.

Miranda watched his technique with admiration. 'And me,' she said. She leaned over Peter's shoulder. 'I like my eggs done on both sides,' she said. 'I hate them when they're all runny.'

'Consider it done,' said Peter, expertly flipping two of the eggs with the spatula. 'These'll be ready in a minute, then we put the lid on to keep it all warm while we heat the beans up.'

'Shouldn't the eggs have been done last?' asked Miranda. 'They'll go all leathery.'

'Whose turn is it to cook?' asked Peter.

'Yours,' said Miranda.

'Correct,' said Peter. 'So mind your own business.'

Miranda retired, muttering to herself about rubbery eggs.

The eggs didn't turn out to be rubbery, and

the three friends ate the meal with relish. They were far too full to set off for Dreath House until later in the afternoon.

Their campsite was at the very southmost rim of Trepolen Moor. The moor stretched out over a wide area. According to their map, a single road crossed it from east to west, although the main through traffic took the motorway several kilometres to the north, well away from the moor.

The moor was stark and bleak but somehow very beautiful at the same time. Standing on the southern ridge and looking away to the distant level horizon in the north, a person could be forgiven for imagining the moor was quite flat and featureless. But it wasn't; it was as rumpled and creased with hills and valleys as an unmade bed. Sheer drops opened unexpectedly and stretches of heather-blanketed moorland which looked flat turned out to have steep slopes.

And then there were the strange standing stones, about two metres tall. They formed three rugged circles and were known as the Dragon Stones. The legend was that these ancient circles were all that was left of three marauding dragons, their bodies turned long ago to lichen-covered stone by a wily wizard.

Gorse, spiny bracken and tufts of purple heather mantled the rugged bones of the moor, plucked up by the raggedy sheep and biscuit-brown cows that dotted the landscape.

As the Mystery Kids walked, a light mist came creeping from the west, giving distant things a hazy, slightly unreal look.

'I think that must be the house,' said Miranda, pointing ahead and slightly to the right. She had insisted on being in charge of the map during this ramble. The other two weren't all that sure about Miranda's map-reading abilities.

They peered at the dark humped shape that lifted on the edge of sight.

'I don't think so,' said Holly. 'It's not house-shaped at all. It's more like a hill.' She took a look at the map. 'It's Butterwrench Tor, you silly thing,' she said. She poked at the map. '*That's* Dreath House, on the far side of the road. We're nowhere near it yet.'

Miranda blinked at the dark Tor. She nodded. 'You could be right. In which case we need to head left a bit.' She squared her shoulders and marched determinedly forwards. 'Follow me! I know what I'm doing.'

Peter and Holly looked at each other and shrugged. With Miranda in charge, this afternoon's ramble could land them anywhere.

'We should be near the road now,' Miranda announced a few minutes later, the map still spread out, completely obscuring her view.

'I think you're right,' said Peter, who could see the way the moor took a sudden dive into a narrow, steep-walled valley only a few metres ahead of Miranda's stomping boots.

'Miranda, watch out,' said Holly as her friend very nearly stalked right over the edge.

Miranda tried to fold the map. In the distance they could see tall black chimneys rising above the curve of a hillside.

'Dreath House!' said Miranda. 'Who says I can't read a map?'

'Hello,' said Peter. 'It looks like someone's in trouble.' He pointed along the road that ran at the bottom of the little valley. Their vision was partially blocked by a large outcrop of rock, but they could see, about thirty metres along the road, that a red car was parked by the roadside, facing them with its bonnet up.

Two men were standing by the front of the car, a third leaning on the open driver's door.

The sound of an approaching car made the Mystery Kids turn their heads. A blue car was coming along, heading towards the broken-down vehicle.

'Perhaps he'll stop to help,' said Holly. 'It can't be much fun breaking down out here.'

As they watched, one of the men from the stationary car stepped into the middle of the road and waved his arms.

The moving car passed the point from which the three friends were watching. It slowed and came to a halt. The driver got out.

To the utter shock of the three friends, two of the men threw themselves on the driver and started dragging him towards their own car. The driver of the first car jumped back in and they heard the motor roar.

There was a brief struggle as the two men forced the driver of the second car into the back.

'Oh, my gosh!' gasped Holly in horrified disbelief. 'They're kidnapping him!'

 **Dreath House**

It had all happened so quickly. One moment Holly and her friends were watching a fairly ordinary scene: a broken-down car and another car stopping to offer help. And the next moment, they were witnessing a kidnapping!

The men bundled into the red car. Urgent shouts cut across the air as the doors were slammed and the motor revved.

'Get the number!' yelled Peter as the car sped towards them. 'Quick!'

It was difficult. They were about ten metres above the road, on the edge of the steep cleft. Miranda was the first to act. She scrambled a little way down the loose scree of stones to try to get a better view of the car's numberplate.

'Careful!' called Holly as she saw Miranda's feet sliding away from under her.

13

'Help!' shrieked Miranda. She lost her balance and went sliding down the slope in a flurry of dust and stones.

Holly jumped down after her. She quickly learned how impossible it was to maintain a foothold on the precarious hillside.

'Oh, heck!' gasped Peter. He sat down on the edge of the slope and pushed off with both hands, using his feet to control his descent as he went sliding down.

Miranda came to a crashing halt by the roadside in a cloud of dust. Pebbles rained down on her as she coughed and spluttered. The red car shot past her, its wheels only centimetres away from her.

There was a shriek of brakes. Holly saw the car half-turn across the road as it came to a grinding halt. The rear doors flew open and the men came tumbling out towards Miranda, who was lying in the road.

Holly had time enough to realise their peril as she hit the road. The men in the car must have realised that the three of them had seen everything. The chances of the Mystery Kids being allowed just to wander off to inform the police didn't look good.

'Leave her alone!' Holly yelled as one of the men leaned over Miranda, his arms stretched out to grab her.

She jumped up and ran forwards. But she didn't get far. Peter came hurtling across her path. There was a moment of tangled legs before Holly, her arms windmilling, fell heavily on to the road.

Someone grabbed Holly's arms from behind and she found herself being lifted bodily off the ground. Hands clenched her upper arms in a fierce vice-like grip. She struggled to get free.

'Keep still, keep still,' said a voice in her ear. 'You'll hurt yourself.' But it wasn't the voice or the powerful hands that brought Holly's struggles to a stop. It was the fact that the kidnapped man, the man from the blue car, was walking towards her across the road.

'Run!' Peter shouted at the man as he too was caught and his arms pinioned at his sides. 'Run! Get away!'

'Check the girl,' said the man from the blue car, gesturing towards Miranda who was still lying dazedly in the road.

The man holding Peter moved towards her.

Miranda sat up, preparing herself to fight for her freedom.

'You touch me and I'll kick you so hard!' Miranda shouted, edging away through the rubble from the approaching man.

Holly saw him grin. 'She's OK,' he said to the man from the blue car.

He approached Holly.

'What are you doing here?' he asked.

'Nothing,' Holly gasped in confusion. Why hadn't the man taken this opportunity to escape? And why had that other man responded to him as though taking orders? 'We thought you were being kidnapped,' she said.

A broad grin spread over the man's face.

He inserted a hand into his jacket pocket and drew out a black wallet. He held his hand up to Holly's face and flipped the wallet open, revealing an official-looking identity card.

'I'm Detective Inspector Truelove,' said the man, snapping the wallet shut while Holly's eyes were still trying to take in what she had been shown. 'And these are my men.'

'Oh!' Holly felt a surge of relief.

'There's no need to hold her,' Inspector Truelove said to the man behind Holly. She was released.

'You're all policemen?' said Peter.

'That's right,' said Inspector Truelove.

Miranda picked herself up and dusted herself down. 'So what the heck were you up to back there?'

'We thought we'd be able to carry out our training programme unobserved,' said the Inspector. 'We didn't exactly plan on having an audience.'

'A training exercise!' breathed Holly. 'You mean – Oh! I get it! You set up a fake kidnapping.'

'We thought it was real,' said Miranda. She gave a loud laugh. Inspector Truelove winced at the unexpected noise. Miranda's laugh took a bit of getting used to.

'I picked this area because I thought we'd be able to work without any interruptions,' said the Inspector. He looked from face to face. 'It seems I was wrong.'

'What are you training for?' asked Peter. 'It seems an odd kind of training exercise.'

The Inspector walked up to Peter and looked him straight in the eyes.

'You don't really expect me to answer a question like that, do you?' said the Inspector. He spun on his heel. 'OK,' he said briskly to the two men, 'let's go. We've wasted enough time already.'

The two men trotted obediently towards the red car where the third man was still waiting in the driving seat.

Inspector Truelove looked at the Mystery Kids. He gave a sudden, surprising wink.

'You can't always judge by appearances,' he told them. 'Remember that.' He smiled. 'And keep out of trouble, OK?'

Before any of them could think of a response, he was off, sprinting back down the road towards the blue car.

The air filled with the noise of revving engines. There was the squeal of brakes as Inspector Truelove came shooting past the three friends.

A brief wave and he was past them, the red car starting off and speeding along in his wake.

'Well,' breathed Peter. 'What did you make of that?'

'A training exercise,' murmured Holly, gazing along the road where the two cars had gone.

'Holly? You OK?' asked Miranda, flapping a hand in front of her friend's eyes.

'Huh?' Holly seemed to snap back to reality. 'I was just thinking, we ought to do things like that.'

'What? Pretend to kidnap each other?' said Peter.

'No, no, no!' said Holly. 'We ought to do training exercises. It's exactly what we need to keep ourselves sharp and really alert.'

'What sort of exercises?' asked Miranda.

'I don't know yet,' said Holly. 'I'll have to think about it.'

'Can we get back to finding Dreath House while you do your thinking?' asked Peter.

They scrabbled up the far bank of the narrow valley. From here the black outlines and tall chimney-stacks of the building they assumed was Dreath House were quite clearly visible through the misty haze.

As they made their way across the last few hundred metres of moorland, Holly was full of ideas for initiative tests and physically-challenging exercises for the Mystery Kids to perform.

'And we could make up exercises to test our reflexes,' she said, getting increasingly excited about the idea. Her two friends looked uneasily at each other behind her back. Once Holly's imagination was rolling, it was difficult to make it stop.

'And other tests,' Holly continued. 'For endurance, and quick-thinking.'

'It's shut,' interrupted Miranda.

'Yes,' said Holly. 'That too.' She stopped and blinked at Miranda. 'What did you say?'

Miranda pointed.

They had circled a shallow rise in the land and Dreath House was directly ahead of them. It was mostly single storey, black and rambling and sinister behind a low stone wall. To the left stood a tall black barn, separated from the main part of the house by a narrow gravel yard.

A standing post displayed a board with 'Dreath House' written on it in gothic script.

The place was completely deserted.

A dirt road ran from a gap in the outer wall, quickly losing itself in folds and tucks

20

of moorland. Peter walked across the track. There was a large sign on top of the wall, giving information about opening times and facilities. Across it was pasted a strip of paper.

' "Closing Down," ' read Peter. ' "Final day of opening to the public – September 12th." '

'But it's still August,' said Miranda.

'September the twelfth two years ago,' said Peter, pointing to the year printed on the strip of paper. 'It's been closed for two years.'

'That's ridiculous,' said Holly. 'Why's it still in the tourist brochures if it's closed down?'

Peter walked back towards them. 'Can I have a look?' he said.

Miranda handed over the crumpled brochure.

'There's your answer,' said Peter. 'This thing is five years old.'

Holly frowned. 'You wait until next time we're in that shop,' she said. 'Fancy selling out of date brochures.' She looked across at the rambling old house. 'I suppose we might as well have a quick look round now we're here,' she said.

They walked in through the gap in the low wall. Dead geraniums straggled miserably from old window boxes. There were a few black benches and tables on the tarmac outside a closed door with 'Restaurant' written over it. Through the grimy windows they could see a large empty room.

'I don't think much of this,' said Miranda as she peered in through another window at yet another empty room.

'I wonder where the Museum of Curiosities was?' said Holly. She walked round a corner and found herself facing another wing of the house. As far as they could see, the only part of the house with two floors was the wing that faced the barn. All the rest stretched out low against the sky under dark, sloping roofs.

They circled the long low wing and came to the back of the house.

'Take a look at this,' said Holly, her face to darkened glass.

Three faces peered in through the window. It was a small room furnished with a simple table and chairs. But on the table were signs of a meal, and lying in one corner of the room was a pile of what looked like blankets or bedding.

'Someone's still here,' said Peter.

'Yeah,' agreed Miranda. 'But it looks kind of makeshift, don't you think?'

She was right. There was half a loaf on the table. There were empty wrappers and opened tins and a scattering of odds and ends, along with a pile of dirty plates and used cutlery and some lager cans.

'Squatters?' suggested Holly. It was all too rough and ready for it to have been a meal provided by a legitimate owner.

'I think you're right,' said Peter. 'Someone's probably seen the place is empty, and they've broken in.'

Holly's shining eyes turned slowly from Peter to Miranda.

'Maybe they're gangsters on the run,' she whispered. 'Maybe we've found the hideout of a band of desperate criminals.'

'Yeah,' Miranda said with a grin. 'All armed to the teeth and ready to cut your throat.' She made a slicing motion of an extended finger across Peter's throat.

Peter rolled his eyes. 'You live in a world of your own sometimes,' he said. 'You really do. Gangsters! Huh!'

An angry bellow from just behind them

made all three of them jump in shock. Holly's head spun round and she let out a scream.

A tall, thick-set man loomed over them, his face contorted with anger and his hands curled into flexing claws.

 **Some exciting news**

The man was all in black, his eyes blazing, a three-day growth of stubble on his chin. He stretched his arms high as though to throw himself at the three terrified friends.

And then his expression changed and he gave a great shout of laughter. He folded his arms and looked at them, his rugged face split by a wide grin.

'That scared you!' he said.

Miranda glared furiously at him, her heart pounding. 'You . . . you . . .' She was almost speechless with indignation.

Holly took a deep, steadying breath. 'That's not very funny,' she managed to croak.

The tall man shrugged. 'I thought it was. Did you think I was a gangster, then?'

'No,' exclaimed Miranda, gathering herself quickly after the initial shock. 'We thought you were a raving lunatic!'

The man looked at her, as if he was wondering how to react to the angry tone of her voice.

Holly thought he didn't look the kind of man who was used to young people talking back to him.

'What are you doing here?' asked the man. 'This place has been closed to the public for years. There's nothing to see.'

'We didn't realise,' said Peter. 'It's still mentioned in our guide. We didn't know it was closed until we got here.'

'So we thought, as we were here anyway,' added Miranda, 'we might as well take a look round.' Her eyes narrowed. 'What's your excuse?'

'Miranda!' Holly whispered warningly.

'I work for the local council,' he said. 'I've been sent out here to do a survey of the place. It may not look it, but it's a dangerous place to hang around.'

'Is it?' said Holly. 'Why?'

There was a pause. 'Rats,' said the man. 'The whole building is infested with rats.' He looked closely at them. 'It's not the sort of place for kids to play near.'

'Kids!' Miranda said affrontedly. 'Of all the—'

'I suppose we'd better get out of here, then,' interrupted Peter. 'Thanks for warning us, sir. We'll go right now.'

Miranda closed her mouth and stared at Peter. Had he gone mad? Neither girl could quite believe it when Peter grabbed them both by an arm and marched them away.

'Peter!' Holly said in a loud whisper. 'What are you doing?'

'Walk,' whispered Peter. 'I'll explain later.'

They rounded the side of the building and made for the gateway in the low wall.

'This had better be good,' said Miranda as Peter towed the two of them across the dirt road and round the hillock that hid them from the house.

At last he released them.

Miranda faced him, her hands on her hips. 'OK,' she said. 'What was all that about? And why did you call that big twit sir?'

''That big twit,' Peter said coolly, 'was the driver of the car on the road back there.'

'Don't be daft,' said Holly. 'That wasn't Inspector Truelove.'

'The *other* car,' Peter said patiently. 'The red car that was supposed to have broken down.'

Holly frowned at him. 'Are you sure?' The driver of the red car had stayed in his seat all the time that Inspector Truelove and the other two men had been with the three friends.

'I'm sure,' said Peter. 'I took a good look at him when we first saw them. He was standing by the car, leaning on the open door. Remember? I saw his face. It was him. Definitely.'

Miranda blinked at him. 'So?' she said, sounding puzzled.

'Don't you get it?' said Peter. 'Can't you work out why he's here?'

'Of course!' breathed Holly. 'They're using Dreath House as a base. It's the perfect secret hideout. If they're on the moor doing training exercises, of course they'd need somewhere as their base. That explains the food and stuff.'

'And it explains that daft story about the rats,' said Peter. 'You could tell he made that up on the spot.'

'He wanted us out of the way so they could carry on with their training in secret,' said Miranda. She gazed at her two friends. 'What on earth can they be in training for? Surely

28

ordinary police officers don't go in for this sort of thing?'

Holly thought for a moment. 'Maybe they're part of a special unit. And there's something else: where was the car? We went just about all the way around the place without seeing it. Which means it's been hidden somewhere.' Her eyes gleamed. 'And why hide the car unless you're up to something top secret?'

'Crumbs,' breathed Miranda. 'A top secret police training exercise – and we've walked right into the middle of it.'

'I think we'd better start walking out of it,' said Peter. 'We could get into trouble.'

'Why?' said Miranda. 'It's a free country, isn't it? We're entitled to be on the moor if we feel like it.'

'Yes,' agreed Holly, 'but we've disturbed them twice already – and they'll be on the lookout for us now they know we're nearby. I think Peter's right.' She took a look at her watch. 'Besides, it's getting a bit late.' She looked at Peter. 'We don't want your dad panicking.' She grinned. 'That'd be the perfect end to the day: having search parties sent out after us.'

\*     \*     \*

They arrived back at camp ahead of Mr Hamilton. The site was a large field, divided into fairly private sections by screens of bushes and trees. There were half a dozen or so other tents dotted about and the friends waved cheerfully to some fellow campers as they headed to the secluded corner where their two small tents were pitched.

'I'll start the food,' said Peter. He opened one of the tents and pulled out a string bag of groceries.

'I'll get the water,' said Miranda.

For the next few minutes Peter and Holly busied themselves peeling and chopping vegetables and opening tins. Everything went into a big pot. It was topped up with the water and put on the gas ring.

'What is it?' asked Miranda, peering into the large pot while Peter added salt and a few herbs.

'It's bean stew,' said Peter.

Miranda screeched with laughter. 'I don't want to know what it's *been*,' she cackled. 'I want to know what it is *now*!'

'That's one for the joke page in *The Tom-tom*,' smiled Holly. *The Tom-tom* was the school magazine which Holly and Miranda co-edited back in London. Holly's favourite section was the mystery page, but Miranda was always on the lookout for terrible jokes.

'I've been thinking,' said Holly as the three of them lounged on the grass round the simmering cooking pot.

'Uh-oh,' said Miranda. 'Here comes trouble.'

'No, listen,' said Holly. 'You know we decided we were going to start doing our own training exercises?'

'We?' said Peter. '*You* decided that.'

Holly gave an airy wave of her hand. 'What we need is some kind of idea of how professionals train. People like Inspector Truelove and his team, I mean.'

'Right,' Miranda said slowly. 'So?'

'Well,' Holly said, sitting up in her eagerness to explain her thoughts. 'I was thinking, maybe we could go back to Dreath House tomorrow and take a look at what they actually do.'

'They'll tell us to push off,' said Peter.

Holly frowned at him. 'I don't mean march up to them and ask if we can watch.' Her eyes lit up. 'It can be our first training exercise. We go over to Dreath House and observe what the Inspector and his men get up to, *without being seen*.' She looked brightly from Peter to Miranda. 'What do you say?'

'It could be fun,' said Miranda.

'And what if they see us?' asked Peter.

'Like Miranda said,' Holly explained, 'it's a free country. There are no signs saying "keep out". There aren't any fences or guard dogs.' She shrugged. 'What can they do if they see us?' A grin spread over her face. 'Besides, if we're really clever – which we are – they won't see us, will they?'

'And maybe we'll get some idea of what they're training for,' said Miranda. 'I'll tell you one thing: Inspector Truelove and his gang are not your average, everyday police officers.'

'I think you're right,' said Holly. 'They're definitely a specialist unit of some sort.'

'I really don't think my dad would be happy about it,' said Peter. 'I'm sure he'll tell us to keep well clear of them.'

'He will if you tell him,' said Miranda.

'I'm not lying to him,' Peter said adamantly.

'No one's saying you should,' said Holly.

'Just don't mention it to him. That's not lying. That's just not telling him everything.'

Peter looked dubiously from Holly to Miranda, but he could already tell by the expressions on their faces that the decision had been made.

'OK,' he said, 'I won't mention it. But you've got to promise not to do anything daft if we do go over to Dreath House.'

'What do you mean, daft?' asked Holly.

'For a start, if we're caught, Miranda's got to promise not to be sarcastic or stroppy with them,' said Peter. 'I can just imagine my dad's face if he has to come and bail us out of prison for obstructing the police in the course of their duties.'

'We won't be caught,' said Holly. 'And if we are, then we'll be polite and reasonable and totally loveable, won't we, Miranda?'

'Of course,' said Miranda. 'Like always.'

Peter shook his head and crawled over to the pot to give the bubbling stew a stir. There were times when being outnumbered two to one could be quite a trial, especially when the two in question were Holly and Miranda!

'Hello, everyone,' called Mr Hamilton. He

came across the grass in his jeans and T-shirt, carrying his briefcase. 'I can smell that food all the way back at the carpark.' He dropped his case and flung himself down on the grass. 'Phew! I'm worn out!'

'Would you like a can of something to drink?' asked Holly.

'I'd love one, thanks,' said Mr Hamilton with a weary grin. 'They've had me pinning up great sheets of canvas all afternoon. I wouldn't mind, but I'm only here as a consultant.'

'Have you got everything finished, though?' asked Miranda. Every night that week, Mr Hamilton had arrived at the campsite complaining that they'd never get the exhibition marquee finished in time for the grand opening on Saturday morning.

Mr Hamilton sat up. 'Very nearly,' he said. 'Believe it or not, I actually think we'll have it all finished in time for the Prime Minister's visit.' He held his hand up, fingers crossed. 'With a bit of luck, that is.'

Holly handed him a can of Coke. 'What was that about the Prime Minister?' she asked.

'Oh, didn't I tell you?' said Mr Hamilton, opening the can. 'The Prime Minister is coming down to open the show on Saturday. Then, apparently, he's going to spend a couple of hours being shown around before leaping into his limousine to go back to London.'

He took a swig of Coke and wiped his mouth with the back of his hand. 'Everyone's going potty about it,' he said. 'All the media will be there. It'll be a big boost for the show.' He grinned. 'And our marquee is right next to the podium where he's going to be making his opening speech. We might even get seen on national television.'

'That's great,' said Peter. 'So will you get to meet him?'

'I hope so,' said Mr Hamilton. He gave the three friends a sly grin. 'I don't suppose any of you three would fancy coming over there with me on Saturday morning, would you? To meet the Prime Minister?'

The yells of astonished delight that greeted Mr Hamilton's question could be heard all over the campsite.

'Oh, wow!' Holly gasped in an ecstasy of disbelief. 'We're actually going to meet the Prime Minister! Oh, *wow*!'

 **4 Undercover work**

Holly woke up early the next morning. She unzipped her sleeping-bag and crawled to the end of the tent. She popped her head out and took a deep breath of the fresh country air. The Mystery Kids had a mission to perform today. A secret mission to Dreath House.

She gave Miranda a wake-up shove with her foot.

Miranda mumbled something and curled deeper into her sleeping-bag, like a hedgehog going into a protective ball.

Holly turned on to her back. Supporting herself on her elbows, she began to rock Miranda from side to side with both feet.

A cross face appeared at the far end of the sleeping-bag.

'I'm awake!' said Miranda.

'Good,' said Holly. 'We've got plenty of work to do today.'

Miranda pulled an arm out of the sleeping-bag and gave her friend a mock salute.

'Anything you say, General Adams.'

Giggling, Holly wormed herself into some clothes and crawled out of the tent. Mr Hamilton was outside, boiling some water.

'Good morning, early bird,' he said. 'Coffee?'

'Yes, please.' Holly padded through the grass to the Portaloos.

By the time she got back, both Peter and Miranda were up and about and Mr Hamilton was getting ready to leave.

'What plans do you have for today?' he asked between rapid slurps of coffee.

'We thought we'd head off across the moor,' said Holly. 'Make a day of it.'

'Don't forget to pack some lunch, then,' said Mr Hamilton. 'And don't get lost!'

'As if!' Miranda laughed.

'I was listening to the weather report on the car radio yesterday evening,' said Mr Hamilton. 'It said there might be fog in this area today.'

'Really?' said Holly, looking up at the brilliant blue sky framed by the tall trees.

Mr Hamilton followed the line of her eyes. 'Don't be deceived,' he warned. 'The weather round here can be very changeable. Take a compass with you, just to be on the safe side.' He patted his pockets, muttering about car keys.

He vanished into the tent that he and Peter shared.

'There's not going to be any fog today,' said Miranda. She looked at Peter. 'Your dad treats us like babies, sometimes, he really does. We've got the map; we don't need a compass.'

Mr Hamilton's head appeared through the tent flap.

'You won't think that if a pea-souper comes down and you end up spending the entire day wandering around lost, young lady,' he said as he crawled out of the tent.

Miranda's face went bright red.

Mr Hamilton smiled at her. 'Here,' he said, holding his hand out to her. He dropped a compass into her palm.

'Sorry,' she stammered.

'No problem,' he said. He picked up his briefcase and set off for the carpark that adjoined the campsite.

'I didn't know he could hear me,' Miranda mumbled.

'With your voice?' said Peter. 'It's like a fog-horn.'

'Maybe we won't need the compass after all,' grinned Holly. 'We can just stand Miranda on a hilltop and get her to shout for help.'

'Are we going to stand here gabbing all day,' Miranda asked crossly, 'or are we going to Dreath House?'

They packed one large rucksack with sandwiches and packets of snacks and cans of drink. Then they added tubes of insect repellant, sting ointment and suntan lotion. Then Peter thought of the small red emergency first aid box. Then Holly thought of sunglasses and some magazines to read.

Finally they were ready.

'Who's got the compass?' asked Peter.

'I have,' said Miranda, patting the back pocket of her jeans. 'Safe and sound.'

'Right,' said Holly, hefting the rucksack on to her back. 'Off we go, then!'

Peter was in charge of the map. Not that they needed it as they headed off over the familiar territory of the southern ridges of Trepolen Moor.

Every now and then Miranda took the compass out, consulted it and pointed authoritatively in the direction in which they were heading anyway.

At first the sun was fierce in a clear sky, stretching long thin shadows out over the moor, but as they headed north, clouds crept over the sky and a faint haze began to develop.

As they passed the Dragon Stones, they looked away over to the right. Butterwrench Tor was a pale misty pool of greyness. The threatened fog was beginning to gather.

They scrambled down to the deserted road and up again.

It wasn't long before they caught sight of the misty chimney tops of Dreath House.

'OK,' said Holly. 'We'd better discuss exactly how we're going to do this.' She took the rucksack off.

'First,' she said, 'we need to suss out the area properly. That means keeping low so we're not seen. We'll have to find ourselves a vantage point to keep watch on the house.'

'How about up there?' said Peter, pointing to the rounded dome of a hillock over to their left.

'Fine,' said Holly. 'Now, keep your heads down. We don't want to be seen against the horizon. That's the worst mistake you can make. I'm going to leave the rucksack here.' She pushed the rucksack under a spiny bush.

The three of them scuttled round to the far side of the hillock then crawled abreast up its long slope.

Three pairs of eyes peered over the crest of the hill. Only a couple of hundred metres away the black shape of Dreath House lay spread out beneath their gaze.

'I've just had a thought,' said Peter. 'If not for the *r* that place would be called Death House.'

Neither of the girls spoke. It wasn't a particularly comforting thought to have in their heads right then. Long tendrils of mist were creeping over the moor, like ghostly fingers exploring and probing the landscape. The name 'Death House' seemed to suit the sombre old building all too well.

There was no sign of life.

'So, what do we do now?' said Miranda after they had been staring down at the house for several minutes. 'Are they in there or not?'

'How should I know?' said Holly. 'The room we saw the food in was round the back, so we won't be able to see them from here.' She scanned the ground round the house. 'We need to get closer.'

'If you ask me, there's no one there,' said Peter. 'I reckon they've gone.'

But Holly wasn't willing to let go of her plans quite that easily. She was much too keyed-up to assume the men had gone away.

'One of us should try to get closer,' said Holly. 'Any volunteers?'

'I volunteer Holly,' said Peter.

'Seconded,' said Miranda.

'I see,' said Holly. 'Thanks very much, *pals*.'

Holly rounded the corner of the house in a crouching run, keeping her head down and moving as quietly as she could.

Ahead of her was the window through which they had seen the debris-strewn table the previous afternoon. It seemed the obvious place to look. Holly had the feeling that maybe Peter was right: maybe Inspector Truelove and his men had gone.

She gradually lifted her head until her eyes rose just over the sash of the window. She let out a slow breath.

The men *were* in the room. They were seated at the table: Inspector Truelove and two of his team. From what Holly could see, the three men were studying a map that lay spread between them.

The Inspector was speaking, but Holly couldn't hear what he was saying. She didn't need to see any more. She ducked down and scampered close to the wall. It was time to report back to her waiting friends.

'They're in there,' she told them breathlessly. 'They were looking at a map. I reckon they're planning the day's activities.' Her heart was beating fast with excitement.

'Where was the fourth man?' asked Peter.

'I don't know,' said Holly. 'I didn't see him.'

'Perhaps he's keeping watch,' said Miranda. Holly nodded. 'Maybe. Look, I've had an idea. We can get to the barn easily enough without being seen from the house,' she said. 'And the barn would be perfect cover for us. We'd be able to see all the comings and goings. We could see which way they go and then follow them.'

'Excuse me,' said Miranda. 'What if they all drive off in their cars?'

Holly stared at her. She hadn't thought of that.

'Well, if that happens we'll have to think of something else to do all day,' said Holly. 'So let's hope they don't.'

As he followed the two girls round the flank of the hill and into the open towards the barn, Peter couldn't help half-hoping that the men would speed off in their cars. He was still far from convinced that this madcap adventure was a good idea.

The main doors to the barn faced the house. If they were going to get inside, it would have to be by some other route. There were no doors in the back, Holly could see that straight away. But there was an old wooden ladder resting against the rear wall. Just above the head of the ladder was a square hole in the black-painted planking that formed the barn's wall.

Motioning for the others to follow, Holly began to climb the ladder. It creaked and swayed alarmingly.

'This is a really rotten idea,' Peter murmured as Miranda took her turn on the precarious old ladder. 'I bet you anything you like, the Inspector and his men are involved in something massively secret. We'll get caught and thrown into the Tower of London. I bet we will.'

'Peter?' said Miranda, looking down at him.

'What?'

'Shut up.'

Holly crawled in through the high entrance and found herself on a gallery that formed a second storey to the barn. It was L-shaped, built half-across the barn. A narrow spur ran along one wall to an opening in the front wall of the barn. The whole structure was supported on massive wooden beams and there was no rail to guard against the four-metre or so fall to the ground. The creaky planking of the floor was strewn with hay and there were rough bales of hay stacked all around.

Maybe the owners of the house used to keep horses here, Holly thought. The barn smelt stale and a little mouldy.

Miranda and Peter followed her and the three of them walked to the front of the gallery. A sheer ladder led down to the similarly hay-covered ground. Directly under them was a large pile of hay, and parked close together near the closed double doors were two cars. The red car and the blue car from the previous day.

'Well,' said Miranda, 'let's take a quick look round.'

She turned and let herself down on to the ladder which led to the ground. Suddenly she stopped and sneezed.

'Ugh!' she spluttered. 'This place is full of dust.'

'Try not breathing,' said Peter.

'Oh, ha, ha,' said Miranda as she made her way down the ladder. She had almost reached the ground when she froze, her head snapping round towards the large barn doors.

They had all heard it. A sharp noise from behind the doors. A noise of someone loosening a chain; and the sound of voices.

Someone was about to enter the barn!

 # The prisoner

The chain that held the barn doors closed rattled again. Miranda stared in silent panic over her shoulder. From the murmur of voices, it was clear that at least two of Inspector True-love's men were about to enter the barn.

She didn't like to think what would happen if they opened the doors to find her perched halfway up the ladder in there.

But she was only frozen into inaction for a moment. She shot back up the ladder as though she'd been fired out of a cannon. Peter and Holly grabbed her and the three of them nose-dived to the boards.

Holly flung a few handfuls of straw over them and then they became as still and silent as hunted animals.

The barn doors opened, letting in a flood of greyish light.

Holly edged nearer to the wooden lip of the gallery. Below her were Inspector Truelove and the man who had told them the story about the house being infested with rats.

The two men approached the blue car.

'Remember what I told you,' said the Inspector as he opened the driver's door. 'He's no fool. Don't take any risks with him.' He climbed into the car. He closed the door and wound down the window.

'Don't worry,' said the other man. 'We're all armed.'

Truelove leaned out of the window. 'Don't be stupid,' he said. 'He's no use to us dead. We still need to know the precise time the target will be crossing the moor.'

'Shall I give him some more of the truth serum?' asked the other man.

'No,' snapped the Inspector. 'We need to give the first dose time to work. A second shot might put him out for hours. Just leave him up there until I get back. Don't do anything, right? That's an order!'

The Inspector started the car and drove it through the barn doorway. The other man followed, pulling the door closed after him.

'Wow,' breathed Miranda.

'Shh!' hissed Holly. 'Stay here!' She wanted to see what would happen next. She pulled herself up and ran lightly to the spur of boards that led to the front of the barn.

She kept in the shadows as she peered round the edge of the high opening. The blue car was passing out through the gap in the outer wall. The other man was walking back to the house.

As they had noticed before, the section of the rambling old house that faced the barn was the only part that consisted of two floors. As Holly stood at her lofty vantage point in the shade of the barn wall, a movement through an upper window of the house caught her eye.

She narrowed her eyes. She was a little bit higher than the window, and perhaps twenty metres away. There were no curtains on the window, but the room beyond was quite shadowy – which made it difficult for her to be sure of exactly what she was seeing. A shape. A dark shape.

And then the shape moved again. It was a man, dressed all in black. He stood briefly at the window, looking down.

The man moved away from the window, back into the interior of the room, and out of the line of Holly's vision. But his disappearance gave Holly the chance to see something else. Something in the room.

A bed. And something – or someone, was lying on the bed. Perfectly still and in a strange, awkward position.

'I knew this was a bad idea.' Peter's anxious voice cut through Holly's concentration. He was having a whispered argument with Miranda.

'Stop flapping like a big wet hen,' said Miranda. 'They didn't see us, did they?'

'But you heard what that man said. They're armed. That means they've got guns!'

'I know what armed means,' said Miranda. 'But they're not going to shoot us for hiding in a barn, for heaven's sake.'

'Holly!' Peter whispered. 'What say we get out of here?'

Holly went back to where her friends were standing.

'I've just seen something odd,' she said. She described the scene in the upstairs room of Dreath House.

'They've got someone held captive up there,' breathed Miranda.

'Someone they've given truth serum to,' said Peter. 'Someone they need to pump for information.' His eyes widened. 'Holly, look, I know you both think I'm a scaredy-cat sometimes, but I really, *really* think we shouldn't be here. It must be something big for the police to be behaving like this.'

'It's odd, though,' said Holly. 'Why would they keep a prisoner locked up out here? Why haven't they taken him to the police station?'

'Maybe they're undercover cops,' said Miranda. 'Maybe the guy on the bed is part of a huge criminal gang that they're trying to capture.' Her voice slowed as she tried to tie up the ends of this idea. 'And . . . er, . . . if they take him to a police station he might, er, they might . . .' She gave an irritated shrug. 'Well, I don't know. There must be some reason.'

'Can we get out of here, please?' said Peter.

'I think Peter's right this time,' said Holly.

Peter let out a gasp of relief. 'Finally! Someone's actually listened to me!'

'Yeah, OK,' Miranda agreed reluctantly. 'Maybe we'll read all about it in the papers in a few days. ''Police uncover vast criminal conspiracy. Entire gang jailed for life.'' ' She sighed. 'I just wish it could read: ''Inspector Truelove admits that entire mission would have failed if not for Miranda Hunt and the other members of the Mystery Kids!'' ' She grinned.

'Not this time,' said Holly. 'I've got the feeling this is too much even for us to tackle. Let's just get out of here.'

'Just one minute,' said Miranda. 'I want to take a quick look at that prisoner they've got in there. Then we'll go.'

'No,' Peter said, grabbing hold of her arm. 'Let's go now!'

'Let go of me,' Miranda snapped, struggling as Peter tried to tow her out of the barn.

'Will you two stop fighting?' said Holly.

But they didn't pay any attention to her. Peter was determined that all three of them should get out; Miranda was equally determined to get her own way and take a look through the upstairs window of Dreath House.

Miranda gave a fierce twist of her arm and

yanked herself loose. The sudden release made her lose balance.

Holly sprang forwards, reaching out as Miranda tottered on the very edge of the gallery floor, her heels in empty air. Miranda arched her back, her arms windmilling.

She just managed to turn as she toppled over the edge, only centimetres away from Holly's clutching fingers.

'Miranda!' Holly wailed as her friend fell.

The barn walls wheeled in front of Miranda's eyes. She twisted herself in the air, hoping to land on her feet. The large heap of straw was directly under her. Perhaps it would break her fall.

*Kerr-rannng!*

The metallic boom echoed through the barn like thunder as Miranda's feet struck against something hard only a few centimetres beneath the blanketing layer of straw. Her feet slid from under her and she crashed heavily on her bottom on to a wide, flat metal surface.

Peter and Holly stared down over the edge of the gallery, their eyes like saucers, the clamour of Miranda's fall loud in their ears.

Miranda couldn't see it: she was too busy

gasping for breath, but Holly and Peter could. The thing she had landed on was a car. The impact of her crash-landing had shaken the straw off the roof and the bonnet.

A sort of quiet descended on the barn and for a few moments everything seemed to be locked in total stillness.

Miranda let out a long moan then climbed down off the roof and sat with a groan in the thick straw.

Holly raced down the ladder, Peter in hot pursuit.

In a matter of seconds they were at Miranda's side.

'Are you OK?' gasped Peter.

'No, I'm not OK,' groaned Miranda. 'I think I've dislocated every bone in my body.'

The complaining tone in Miranda's voice filled Peter and Holly with relief. If she was able to moan about it, then she couldn't be that badly hurt.

They grabbed an arm each and heaved her to her feet.

'Ow!' she yelped. 'Ow! Oh, crumbs! I think I've broken my bottom!' She pulled her arms free and rubbed the seat of her jeans. 'It's going to be black and blue. I'm never going to be able to sit down again. Oh, crumbs!'

She turned and gave the half-hidden car a devastating glare. 'What a totally, completely and utterly stupid place to put a car!' she exclaimed, giving the bumper a fierce kick. 'Ow!' She hopped about on one leg, cradling her foot in both hands.

'Calm down,' said Peter.

'I'm in pain!' groaned Miranda, plumping down in the straw.

'This is very strange,' said Holly, staring at the grey car. 'Why on earth should anyone hide a car under all this straw?'

'So no one would know it was there,' said Peter. 'That's obvious.'

'Yes, but why only hide one car?' asked Holly. 'Surely you either hide the lot or don't bother hiding any of them. I don't get it.' She circled the car, kicking her way through the straw until she got to the driver's door.

A black briefcase lay on the driver's seat.

'Maybe it belongs to the man they've got held captive up there,' said Peter, also having a look.

Holly tried the handle. The door opened.

Miranda's groans subsided as she and Peter were drawn to where Holly was leaning into the car.

Holly turned the case and flicked the two metal locks with her thumbs. They sprang open with a sharp click.

Holly opened the case. It held folders of documents, not unlike the sort of official papers that filled her own father's briefcase. There were a few loose letters and single printed sheets, some of which had an impressive crest on the top.

A black leather wallet lay on top of the folders.

She opened the wallet. On one side was an identity card. It showed a photo of a thin-faced, dark-eyed man with a receding hairline.

As her two friends leaned over her shoulders, Holly read the wording on the card.

' "Detective Inspector Alec Truelove. Special Security Division," ' she read breathlessly. ' "Security Level A. Access to all areas. Licensed to carry firearms." '

'This isn't Inspector Truelove,' said Miranda, forgetting all her aches and pains for a moment.

The middle-aged, lined and weather-beaten

face which gazed back at them was of a total stranger.

Holly swallowed. 'But if the real Inspector Truelove is the man in this photo,' she said softly, 'then who's that other man?'

 **Peter in peril**

'Plastic surgery,' said Miranda. 'That's the answer. He's had plastic surgery to keep his identity a secret.'

''That's ridiculous,' said Peter. 'They're not in the least bit similar.'

Miranda put her hands on her hips. 'That's the whole point of plastic surgery,' she said. 'You're supposed to come out looking totally different!'

'But look,' Peter insisted, brandishing the identity card under Miranda's nose. 'This man has got a much thinner face. And a smaller nose and different coloured eyes. His face is a completely different shape. To make the man in this photo look like the guy who just drove off out of here, he wouldn't need plastic surgery, he'd need a head transplant!'

Miranda turned to her other friend. 'Holly?

You've gone very quiet. What do you think? He's had plastic surgery, hasn't he? I'm right, aren't I?'

'I don't think so,' Holly said slowly. 'Peter's right. I really don't think plastic surgery could make that much difference. It's a different man.'

Miranda's face registered alarm as this thought finally hit home. 'But if he isn't Inspector Truelove,' she said, 'then none of them can be policemen. So who are they? And what are they?'

'If they're not the good guys,' said Peter, 'there's only one thing they can be.'

'Oh, heck!' said Miranda.

'And I've got a pretty good idea who it is that they're holding hostage up in that room,' said Holly. 'The real Inspector Truelove.'

'We need to get help,' said Peter. 'And quick!'

They froze as a muffled voice sounded from beyond the doors. At first they couldn't make out what was being said, but they could tell that the owner of the voice was approaching the barn.

'I think it came from in here,' said the voice, now much nearer. 'Keep me covered.'

'Hide!' whispered Holly. It wasn't difficult to work out what had happened. The men in the house had heard Miranda's crash. They were coming to investigate – and by the sound of it they were coming with guns at the ready.

The three friends only had a few moments to react. The doors had not been chained again after the departure of the bogus inspector's car. A couple of seconds and the huge wooden door would be swinging open.

Holly dived on to her stomach and clawed her way under the grey car. With a muffled yelp, Miranda ran for a pile of old sacks heaped in one corner of the barn. She did a nose-dive over them and pulled them on top of her. The sacks stank!

Peter shoved the Inspector's identity card in his pocket. He needed somewhere to hide. The other car! The red car. If he could worm his way under it, like Holly had done with the grey car, he'd be safe.

He ran for it and threw himself on to the straw-covered floor. Stretching his arms out, he wriggled and writhed through the straw, pulling himself in under the rear bumper.

The barn door creaked open.

Peter felt something snag in his belt. He twisted his head round and saw that he'd got himself tangled up with the exhaust pipe. His legs were still visible. Stifling a groan of despair, he tried to wrench himself free.

Something caught his ankles. He struggled vainly for a few moments as he was steadily drawn out from under the car.

He was picked up by the scruff of his neck. An angry face glowered at him.

'What are you doing here?' It was the same man who had startled them yesterday afternoon. The man who had told them the place was crawling with rats.

Peter swallowed hard, trying to think through the pounding of blood that sang in his ears.

'I'm interested in cars,' he gasped. 'I wasn't doing any harm.'

A second man came into the barn. He was wielding a gun, but when he saw Peter in the first man's grasp, he slid it into a shoulder holster and walked over to them.

'What's this?' he said. 'What's going on?'

'I'll ask you once more,' the first man said to Peter. 'What are you doing in here?'

Peter went limp. He had come up with an idea. But would it work? 'It was a dare,' he said. 'They dared me to come back here.' He blinked innocently at the men. 'So I had to, didn't I? It was a *dare*.'

'Who dared you?' asked the second man.

'Those two girls,' said the first man, still keeping a tight grip on Peter's collar. 'That's who you mean, isn't it?'

'That's right,' said Peter. 'They dared me I wouldn't come back here – after what you said yesterday about the rats. They dared me to come inside.'

'Where are they?' asked the first man.

'Where are who?' Peter said, playing dumb.

'The girls, you little fool. Where are the girls?'

'Oh, them,' said Peter. 'They're back at the campsite.' He waved a vague arm. 'I came here on my own.'

'I see,' said the second man. He walked over

to the grey car and ducked his head in through the open driver's door. Peter glanced uneasily at him.

It only took the man a second or two to see the open briefcase and the wallet with the identity card missing. He walked over to Peter.

'Where is it?' he asked.

Peter put his hand in his pocket and pulled out the card.

The second man drew the gun from inside his jacket, but the first man shook his head.

'Wait until Ray gets back,' he said. 'I'm not taking responsibility for this.' He looked hard into Peter's face. 'I'll give you a word of advice, boy: don't take risks just to show off to girls. That's a bad habit to get into.'

'Wh–what are you going to do?' Peter stammered. 'You're not going to phone the police, are you? I wasn't doing any harm, honest. My dad'll be really mad at me if I'm not back at the campsite in half an hour.'

The first man almost grinned. 'Don't worry,' he said. 'We're not going to call the police.' The two men looked at each other and exchanged a harsh laugh.

They marched Peter to the door.

'My dad'll wonder where I am,' Peter said desperately. 'And the girls are bound to tell him. He'll probably be here any minute.'

The last thing Holly heard as the barn doors were swung shut was one of the men saying, 'You'd better hope he *doesn't* come here looking for you.'

There was a dull clank of the chain being put back in place and then the muffled crunch of feet on gravel which faded to an uneasy silence.

Holly edged herself out from under the car and ran to where she had seen Miranda hide.

The filthy old sacks reeked. Holly dragged them away until Miranda was revealed, curled up deep in the corner, one arm cradled over her head, her eyes shut tight and the fingers of her other hand clamped on her nose.

Holly shook her. Miranda's eyes sprang open and she let out a pent-up breath.

'Have they gone?' she gasped.

'They've taken Peter!'

'What?'

Holly pulled Miranda out of her foul nest. 'They've gone off with Peter.' Covered in the sacks, Miranda hadn't been able to hear a thing. Holly quickly told her what had happened.

'We've got to rescue him,' Miranda said without a moment's hesitation.

'Of course,' said Holly. 'But what do you think's going on here? These men have kidnapped the real Inspector Truelove and are holding him hostage here. But why?'

'For money?' suggested Miranda.

'Ransom money, you mean?' said Holly. 'I don't think so, somehow. I think it's got something to do with him working for a special security division of the police.'

'I've just realised!' said Miranda. 'I know what they were up to the first time we saw them. They were practising a kidnapping. They were rehearsing how they were going to grab the inspector.'

Holly nodded, remembering the fleeting way she was shown the identity card of the man who had called himself Inspector Truelove; the man the others had just revealed was called Ray. She hadn't been given time to actually see what was printed on the card. Now she knew why. They didn't have the card at that time. They must have captured the Inspector some time *after* their encounter with the three friends.

'How long do you think it would take us to get help?' asked Holly.

'The nearest place must be the campsite,' said Miranda. 'Even if we ran all the way, it'd take . . . I don't know . . . half an hour or more.' Her jaw set determinedly. 'Anyway, I'm not running away and leaving Peter with these weirdos.'

'You're right,' said Holly. 'We can't abandon him like that. And maybe there's a phone in the house. Maybe we can sneak in and call for help from there?'

'A phone?' Miranda said dubiously. 'I'd have thought the phone would have been cut off ages ago.' Her face brightened a little. 'Still,' she said, 'they might have one of those mobile phones. It's got to be worth a try.'

'OK,' said Holly. 'Here's what we do. We find a way into the house. If there is a phone we call the police and then sit tight until they arrive. And if there isn't a phone, we rescue Peter and make a run for it.'

'And phone the police as soon as we get

back to the campsite office,' added Miranda. She nodded. 'Agreed!'

The barn doors had been chained again so the two girls made their way up the ladder to the upper floor. They climbed out and carefully descended the rickety ladder to the ground at the rear of the barn.

Holly led the way as they edged along the side of the barn until they were in sight of the black house.

They made whispered plans of attack. They needed to find an unlocked window or door, preferably somewhere a fair distance away from that room where Holly had seen the men.

They ran swiftly to the house and plastered themselves against the wall, their ears straining for any sound. Holly raised an encouraging thumb to Miranda and began to edge along the wall. The first window they came to was locked tight.

They continued their stealthy prowl along the wall.

And then Holly found it. A tall, narrow window that wasn't quite shut. Peering through the dusty glass she could see that the catch was broken away. It took both of them all their strength to prise the window open.

Holly climbed on to the sill and edged herself in through the thin windowframe. She found herself in a hallway. She listened for a few seconds then beckoned for Miranda to follow.

Miranda wriggled through the narrow gap and jumped down inside.

Holly stifled a yell as Miranda landed heavily on her foot.

'Sorry,' mouthed Miranda.

They padded along the hallway, ready to run for it at the slightest sound. The hall took a sharp bend and widened. At the far end were a pair of doors with decorated glass panels. Lining the hall on either side were three closed doors.

Holly crouched at the first keyhole. Framed by blackness she saw a medium-sized room. It was completely empty and there wasn't even a carpet on the floor.

Following her example, Miranda explored the keyholes along the other side. The first room was painted a really sickly green and had no furniture in it. There was a piano in the second room, and a pile of chairs against one wall.

In the third room, caught squarely in the frame of the keyhole, Peter sat tied to a chair with a gag round his mouth.

Miranda gave a squeak and flapped her hand at Holly. As Holly slid across the hallway, Miranda took a second look through the keyhole, angling her head to try and make certain that there was no one in the room with Peter.

Miranda stood up, took a deep breath, and turned the handle.

The door opened. Peter's head snapped round and a look of such joy and relief came over his face that Miranda couldn't help but give a soft whoop of 'Yessss!'

Holly pushed her in and closed the door behind them. She ran over to where Peter sat in a tangle of well-knotted ropes. She tugged down his gag. Peter gave a gasp.

'You took your time!' he said.

Miranda's fists came up to her hips. 'Well, I like that,' she said. 'Who was daft enough to get caught in the first place?'

'There's no time for all that,' said Holly. She

crouched behind Peter and started picking at the knots. 'We've got to get out of here!'

The knots were fiendish, but slowly Holly and Miranda began to get them loose.

'You'll soon be free,' grinned Miranda. 'Nothing can go wrong now.'

As though in response to her words, the sound of a heavy footfall echoed in the hallway.

It seemed that Miranda had spoken too soon.

# **7** Bound and gagged

The two girls stared at each other across the knotted ropes that held Peter fast in the chair. Someone was about to enter the room. They had to hide or risk capture.

But this wasn't like the barn. There were no cars to slip under. No pile of sacks to dive behind. There were no hiding-places at all. They were in a room about four metres square without enough cover to hide a mouse!

Holly glanced round. Apart from the door, the only other exit was via the window, and there was no time to escape that way, with or without Peter. And then she saw that there was one hope. A faint one, admittedly, but even a faint hope was better than just standing there.

She snatched at Miranda's hand and dragged her across the room. Holly pulled them both to one side of the already opening door. The hinge side. The door opened inwards. If the man left the door open, then the two girls would be hidden behind it.

The door swung fully open and the man who had told them about the rats walked into the room. He was holding something quite small. A sort of tube, Peter thought, although he couldn't make out exactly what it could be.

From the corner of his eye, Peter could see Miranda's shoulder and arm showing from behind the wide open door. He switched his gaze to the man's face. He knew he had to keep his eyes firmly away from that part of the room. The man only had to look round, and the girls would be caught.

The man's face contracted into a narrow-eyed frown.

'So,' he said softly as he approached Peter. 'You got the gag off, did you?' He smiled unpleasantly. 'That's good, because I want you to be able to talk.'

Peter realised that from the front there was no sign that his bonds had been loosened.

'My father will be here looking for me any

time now,' Peter said, as steadily as he could. 'If you don't let me go, you're going to be in really bad trouble.'

'I don't think so,' said the man. He lifted his hand and showed Peter what he was holding. It was a syringe. The sort of syringe that doctors use to give injections of medicine. 'Do you know what this is?'

Peter stared in shock at the syringe. It was filled with a pale, yellowish liquid.

'No.'

'It's truth serum,' said the man. 'You see, I don't think you were telling the truth back there. I don't think you came back here because those girls dared you. I think you came to spy on us.' The man's eyes became stony. 'I don't like being lied to.'

Peter watched in horror as the man leaned over him and the needle came closer.

A sound from outside the house made the man stop. He lifted his head, tilting it as though listening. Peter could hear it as well. The crunch of wheels on gravel and the growl of a motor.

'Ray,' murmured the man, his face clouding. 'Damn!'

He straightened up, looking down at Peter.

'We'll have to postpone our little chat,' he said as he jerked the gag back up over Peter's mouth. 'Just for a while.'

Peter slumped in relief as the man slammed the door and the horrified faces of his two friends were revealed.

Peter struggled, making frantic noises as Holly and Miranda ran forwards.

'Wait,' said Holly, taking hold of Miranda's arm as she headed for the back of the chair to continue undoing the ropes. 'This may not be the best thing to do.'

Peter's eyes almost popped as he stared at her.

'What do you mean?' whispered Miranda. 'We've got to get Peter out of here. You heard what that rat was going to do.'

'Yes, the "Rat" is a good name for him. But he stopped when he heard his boss's car arrive,' said Holly.

'So what?' said Miranda. 'Do you think Ray is going to pat Peter on the head and send him home?'

'No, of course not,' said Holly. 'But he's bound to want to see Peter straight away.

If we release him now they'll know we're nearby. They'll probably catch the whole lot of us.'

Peter made strangulated noises and shook his head around.

'So what do we do?' asked Miranda.

'Leave Peter here until Ray has seen him,' said Holly. 'Then we can come back and set him free.'

'And in the meantime we can search for a phone,' said Miranda. She looked at Peter. 'It makes sense,' she said, seeing the panic in his eyes. 'And we'll be back before you know it. Honestly.' Miranda knelt beside him and tightened the knots that the two girls had fought so hard to loosen.

'Just in case anyone notices,' she said, getting up.

'*Mmrrghhh! Urrgh murrgh!*' Peter writhed in his bonds, his eyes bulging as his two friends edged to the door. It might make sense to them, but from Peter's point of view, being left there at the mercy of those men was not a good idea at all!

Miranda suddenly ran back and gave Peter a quick peck of a kiss on the forehead. 'We'll set you free really soon,' she said. 'Just be brave for a few more minutes.'

And then they were gone. Peter stared disbelievingly as the door closed quietly on his two friends. They'd left him! They'd walked out and left him tied and gagged and at the mercy of four armed men.

'I feel terrible,' Holly whispered as the two girls crept along the hallway. 'Poor Peter!'

'It was your idea to leave him,' said Miranda.

'I know,' said Holly. 'That doesn't make me feel any better about it.' She paused at the glass-panelled doors and edged her eyes up. The room beyond was large, the walls stacked with tables and chairs.

She recognised it. It was the restaurant at the front of the building. They were some distance from that back room where they had first seen signs that the house was occupied.

And then Holly saw a pay-phone attached to the wall just beyond the doors.

She pushed through the doors and lifted the receiver, her finger poised to dial 999. But her grin of triumph faded as she put the receiver to her ear. It was silent. The line was dead.

'Did you really think there'd still be a phone line after two years?' said Miranda on hearing the news.

'I suppose not,' sighed Holly. 'I just *wished*.'

'So, now our only hope is that those men have a mobile phone and that somehow we can get our hands on it.' Miranda's forehead wrinkled. 'It doesn't sound too likely, does it?'

'Not really,' said Holly. 'I think we'd better forget trying to phone from here. Let's just free Peter and get away.'

'I want to show you something,' said Miranda. The hallway took a sharp bend to the right, following alongside the wall with the restaurant doors in it. At the end of this short spur were two doors and a window.

As she followed her friend, Holly thought the window must be very dirty: she could hardly see through it at all. It was as opaque and as grey as . . .

'Fog!' said Miranda as the two of them stared out through the window into a dense wall of swirling grey nothingness.

'Oh, crumbs,' breathed Holly. 'Where did that come from?'

'We saw it heading our way ages ago,' said Miranda.

'Yes, but not this thick,' said Holly, straining to make out anything at all through the enveloping blanket of fog. But all she could see was the ground directly under the window; ground which faded rapidly into invisibility. It was as if the world ended two metres beyond that window.

'But it's just what we need,' said Miranda. 'It would have been a total nightmare, trying to get away from those men in clear daylight. But in this, they'll never find us.' She patted her back pocket, wincing a little at the soreness since her fall. 'And we've got a compass, thanks to Peter's dad.'

'OK,' said Holly. 'Here's the deal. We wait a few minutes, until—' Her voice cut off abruptly. From round the bend of the hallway they could hear the sound of footsteps and voices.

'Are you sure there wasn't anyone else with him?' That was Ray's clipped, precise voice.

'We didn't see anyone else,' came the voice of one of the other men.

'Did you make a thorough search of the area?' asked Ray.

'Well, we—' That was the voice of the man Holly now thought of as the Rat. The man who had threatened Peter.

'It didn't seem necessary,' cut in the voice of the other man.

'Didn't it?' Ray said icily. 'He was with two girls before. Are you certain they're not hanging around? If the boy disappeared suddenly, don't you think they'd look for him?'

'I'll send Frank out to check,' said the man.

'No, you won't,' said Ray. 'All three of you will make certain there's no one out there anywhere.'

'But the fog . . .' said the Rat.

'That was an order, Sergeant,' said Ray. 'I'll talk to the boy. You two, pick up Frank and search for those two girls. We're too close to Zero Hour to start slacking off now.'

'Yes, sir.'

Holly and Miranda stared at each other as they heard the sound of retreating footfalls. There was the sound of a door opening and then closing. They didn't need to have seen anything to know what had happened. The two men had marched off, and Ray had gone into the room where Peter was tied up.

'Did you hear that? He called him sergeant,' Miranda whispered. 'Do you think they're something to do with the army?'

'Maybe,' Holly said softly. 'But not necessarily *our* army.'

Miranda's eyebrows shot up as her eyes became round. 'You mean, a foreign army?' she gasped. 'You think they're something to do with an army from a different country?'

'I don't know,' said Holly. 'But their boss said they were close to Zero Hour, which means that whatever is going to happen, it's going to happen soon.'

'So kidnapping Inspector Truelove is only part of it,' breathed Miranda. 'Holly, what on earth are they up to?'

Holly put her finger to her lips and sidled to the corner. She jerked a rapid glance down the hallway then ducked back.

'Here's the plan,' she whispered to Miranda. 'We wait here until the boss has finished talking to Peter. As soon as he leaves the room, we get back in there, let Peter loose, and make a run for it.'

Miranda nodded her agreement and the two girls rested against the wall, their ears pricked for the sound of the door opening.

They didn't have long to wait. A minute later they heard the door open and close again. Footsteps faded away as the two girls held their breath.

Holly counted to fifty before daring a swift glance down the hall. It was deserted.

'Right,' she whispered to Miranda. 'Free Peter, and we're out of here!'

They glided, silent as a pair of ghosts, along the hallway to the door of the room where Peter was being held captive.

Holly made a thumbs up sign to Miranda as she turned the handle. Two minutes – five at the most, and the three Mystery Kids would be out of Dreath House and heading across the fog-bound moor towards the nearest telephone.

The door creaked a little as she opened it.

'It's OK, Peter,' she said in a loud whisper. 'We're back. We've come to . . . oh! Oh, *no*!'

Startled by her friend's despairing groan, Miranda peered round Holly's shoulder. The chair was still there, and lengths of rope were coiled on the floor.

But Peter was gone.

# 8 The real Inspector Truelove

*I had a bad feeling about this from the very start,* Peter thought as he stared at the closed door through which his two friends had just left the room. *I should never, never listen to those two!*

He used up a lot of energy straining at the ropes that bound him to the chair. There were ropes looped round his waist that pulled him tight back in the chair. There were more ropes tying his ankles to the chair legs, and another lot of rope wrapped round his wrists and somehow secured to the back of the chair.

And there was a wound-up length of material up over his mouth as a gag. He tried working it loose by opening and closing his jaw, but it didn't make any difference.

There was nothing he could do except sit there, and hope the girls came back to rescue him before that maniac with the syringe turned up again. There was something in that man's eyes that Peter found very alarming.

Peter looked round his prison. Bare walls. A bare floor. Not a stick of furniture except the chair he was sitting in. But there had to be some way of escaping. All he had to do was work it out.

And then he heard voices just outside the door. Not the longed-for voices of Holly and Miranda. Male voices.

The door opened and the man called Ray walked in. He wore a shoulder holster and Peter could see the butt of a revolver sticking out from under his arm. He closed the door behind himself and walked towards Peter.

'Well,' Ray said, folding his arms. 'That was very silly of you, wasn't it? Getting caught.' He reached out and gently eased the gag down. 'The question is: what are we going to do with you?'

Peter took a deep breath. 'Look,' he said, 'I don't know why you've tied me up, but my friends know I'm here. They're going to start worrying if I'm not back soon. People are going to come here to see what's happened to me.'

Ray looked thoughtfully at him.

'That may well be true,' he said, walking over to the window and staring into the fog. 'But I don't think you were altogether honest with my men earlier. Now then, what was your story? The girls sent you over here on a dare, and they're back at some campsite or other?' Ray came away from the window and slowly circled Peter as he spoke.

'You see, I don't think that's what happened,' Ray continued. He crouched behind Peter and started to loosen his bonds. 'I think all three of you came over here.'

Peter felt the ropes slacken and Ray came round to face him.

'Your friends didn't strike me as the sort of girls who'd send someone off to do something daring,' said Ray as he knelt to untie Peter's ankles. 'I think they'd want to be in on it. I think both of them came with you, but only you got caught. Am I getting a little closer to the truth?'

'Not at all,' said Peter. 'If they'd been in the barn, your men would have caught them.'

Ray laughed softly as he unlooped the ropes from round the chair-leg.

'You've got more confidence in them than I

have,' said Ray. He began to unwind the ropes from round Peter's waist. 'But you don't have to give your friends away. I'm sure enough in my own mind that they were with you. And maybe they have gone for help, but it'll be a while before they get anywhere, especially in this fog.'

'What are you doing here?' asked Peter. 'Why are you holding Inspector Truelove hostage?'

Ray stared at him. 'How did you know that? Ahh! Of course. The identity card.' He caught hold of Peter's jacket and pulled him to his feet. 'Can you stand? Have your legs gone numb?'

'I'm OK,' said Peter. 'Are you going to tell me what all this is about? I know you're not with the police – that's obvious. Are you something to do with MI5?'

'No.'

'The army, then?' persisted Peter. 'The SAS?'

'I suppose you could say we're a military taskforce,' said Ray. He put his hands on Peter's shoulders and leaned over, staring into his eyes. 'But before you decide to ask

86

any more questions, let me tell you one thing. If I thought for a moment you or your friends knew what our mission was, I'd have had you shot dead the moment you were seen.' He gave a grim smile at the look of shock that came over Peter's face. 'Any further questions?'

Peter shook his head, his mouth clamped tight shut.

'Good,' said Ray. 'I thought not.' His fingers closed round Peter's collar. 'If you behave yourself I promise that no harm will come to you. We've come here to do a job, and once that job's done, we'll be gone. But we can't afford to let you go until we're clear of the area.' A push from behind propelled Peter towards the door. 'I think it'll be much safer if we keep the two of you together.'

Ray smiled at Peter's puzzled expression.

'I'm taking you to meet the real Inspector Truelove,' he said.

Peter was led into the hallway by a firm hand on his back.

He soon lost track of the route they were taking. He wondered whether Holly and Miranda were silently following at a discreet distance. If not, he wondered how long it would take the two girls to find him.

He hoped now that they would decide to go for help. The other three men might just be dangerous thugs, but their leader seemed all-too intelligent. He didn't seem the sort of man who could be outsmarted even by Holly's quick thinking.

They came to a flight of stairs. Now Peter knew where he was; they were in that part of Dreath House that faced the black barn. He was near the room where the hostage was being held. That upper room where Holly had seen the captive on the bed.

They mounted the stairs and Peter was pushed into a room. There was a chair and a cabinet; and along one wall, a metal bed with a bare mattress. A man lay stretched out on the bed, facing towards the wall, his arms above his head, secured by handcuffs through which a chain had been looped. The chain was wound round the bedhead and padlocked.

The man didn't stir or make any sound as they entered.

'Sit there,' ordered Ray, pointing to the chair. Peter sat down. Ray took a thick roll of black sticky tape from the top drawer of the cabinet and began to tape Peter into the chair.

'Don't waste your energy trying to get free,' said Ray. 'This tape could hold an angry gorilla.' He produced a knife and cut the tape, leaving Peter cocooned into the chair. But at least this time there was no gag, and his arms were in front of him rather than pulled behind.

As Peter watched, Ray walked over to the bed and sat down on the edge of it. He reached over and turned the docile man on to his back. Peter recognised the face. There was stubble and the sallow, sunken-eyed look of sleep-deprivation, but Peter could see that the man on the bed was the same man in the photo on the identity card they had found in the grey car. It was Inspector Truelove.

Ray lightly slapped the man's face.

'Come on, come on, my friend,' he said softly. 'Time to wake up now.'

The man groaned and his dark-rimmed eyes fluttered open.

'That's better,' said Ray, his voice gentle and coaxing. 'Now then, all I want is a little piece of information.'

'Sleep,' murmured the man. 'Let . . . me . . . sleep.'

'Soon,' said Ray. 'You can sleep very soon.' He patted the man's cheek again. 'Stay awake, my friend. Just for a few more moments. Then you can sleep for as long as you like. Can you hear me? Can you understand what I'm saying?'

'Yes,' gasped the man.

'Good,' crooned Ray. 'That's very good. Now, just tell me what time his car will be crossing the moor. That's all I want to know.'

'I don't know . . . what car . . . you mean . . .' gasped the man, his head turning from side to side.

'You're being difficult, my friend,' said Ray, a hint of cold steel entering his voice. 'Now, you wouldn't want us to have to give you another dose of that serum, would you? We'd get the information then, all right, but you might not survive the experience.' The voice softened again. 'Don't fight it, my friend. The sooner you tell me what I want to know, the sooner I let you go to sleep. Now then, look at me.' He caught the delirious man's chin in his hand and leaned close over him, almost eyeball to eyeball with him. 'What time is the Prime Minister's car going to be crossing Trepolen Moor?'

The truth of what these men were planning to do on the moor finally hit Peter with a shock like a faceful of icy water. The Royal West Country Show opened tomorrow morning. The Prime Minister would be coming down from London to give an opening speech. And there was only one reason Peter could think of why these men would want to know precisely when the Prime Minister's car would be crossing Trepolen Moor. And that was so they could ambush it on that quiet stretch of road.

'Friday evening,' murmured the drugged Inspector. 'The Prime Minister's car is scheduled to cross Trepolen Moor early on Friday evening.'

'What!' Ray's voice rose to a shout. He slapped the Inspector's face. 'Not Saturday morning? Dammit! I didn't think he'd be travelling down here today!' He grabbed the Inspector's shoulders and shook him hard. 'What time? What time on Friday evening?'

'Between six . . . and . . . seven . . .' gasped the Inspector.

Ray leaped up from the bed. He took one glance at his watch, let out a stream of swearing, and ran for the door.

Peter lifted his bound hands. The sticky tape criss-crossed over his watch, but a section of the face was still visible. Enough for him to see that the hands on his watch showed half past four.

No wonder Ray had moved so quickly. One and a half hours from now the Prime Minister's car could be driving across the moor. And unless there was some way for Peter to let someone know what he had just heard, there would be an armed gang waiting somewhere along the route.

Waiting to hijack the Prime Minister's car.

 **Revelations**

Peter's head reeled as he listened to Ray's footsteps hurrying down the stairs. He could hardly believe what he had just heard. But it was true! Ray and his men were here to do something to the Prime Minister's car as it crossed the moor.

And the car would be crossing the moor in a couple of hours. Peter strained and heaved, but the sticky tape held him fast.

Inspector Truelove was lying stretched out, his eyes closed, mumbling to himself.

'Inspector Truelove!' Peter called softly. 'Hey! Inspector!'

The drugged man's head turned jerkily from side to side.

'I know what's going on,' said Peter. He writhed frantically in his bonds. The chair tipped and nearly overbalanced.

'Inspector!' he said. 'Look, I'm going to

try and get closer to you.' Peter's forehead wrinkled. The man showed no sign of understanding a word he was saying. 'Maybe you can help untie me.'

It was a desperate hope. Peter threw his weight from side to side, gradually edging the chair closer to the bed. A determined frown gathered on Peter's face. He wrenched his shoulders around, swinging his arms.

It was working. He only hoped that Ray and his men were far enough away not to be able to hear the screech of the chair legs on the bare boards as Peter edged himself slowly closer and closer to the bed.

Finally, Peter's knee bumped against the side of the bed.

'Inspector!' he said. 'Help me!'

Bleary eyes opened and tried to focus on Peter. The man's face was running with sweat.

'Must . . . warn . . . base . . .' murmured the Inspector. 'Terrorists . . .'

'Yes, I know,' said Peter. 'They've given you some sort of drug. You told them the Prime Minister's car was going to be crossing the moor.'

'The Prime Minister!' gasped the Inspector. He lifted himself a little off the bed and then fell back with a groan. 'I'm not going to tell you anything,' he gasped.

'I'm not them,' Peter said in desperation. 'Hello! Inspector! Please! You've got to try and understand what I'm saying.'

He simply had to make the delirious man understand.

'Inspector!' he said sharply. 'Listen to me. You've already told them what they wanted to know.'

For the first time, the man's gaze flickered across Peter's face and held. A glimmer of understanding ignited in his eyes.

'Try to think,' urged Peter.

'Where . . . am . . . I?'

Peter almost felt like crying out with relief. 'You're being held captive in Dreath House on Trepolen Moor. It's Friday afternoon.'

'Friday?' mumbled the Inspector, shaking his head. 'No. Thursday.'

'They've drugged you,' said Peter. 'Do you understand what I'm saying?'

The Inspector's eyes narrowed. 'Who are you?'

'I'm Peter Hamilton, but it doesn't matter,' said Peter. 'You've got to help me get free.

Don't you realise? You told them about the Prime Minister.'

A shaft of comprehension seemed to enter the man's eyes.

'He's crossing . . . the moor . . . between . . . six and seven in the evening . . . on Friday,' mumbled the Inspector.

'I know!' wailed Peter. 'And so do *they*! And it's already gone half past four! That's why I've got to get free.'

The Inspector's forehead creased as he tried to think. Inspector Truelove seemed to be gradually gathering his wits, but it was taking far too long.

'Can you try and get my hands loose?' asked Peter, holding his arms out over the bed. The Inspector's head lolled forwards.

'Get help,' he muttered. The chain rattled as he pulled his arms down.

'I will if you help me get free,' said Peter. He rocked to and fro, angling the chair so that he could bring his hands closer to the Inspector. 'Can you just pull at the end of the tape?'

'I'll . . . try,' gasped the Inspector. He stretched his cuffed hands down and picked at the trailing end of the tape. After a few moments he managed to take hold of the end of it.

'Just hold it,' said Peter. 'I'll do the rest.'

Peter slowly circled his wrists, unpeeling the tape centimetre by centimetre. The Inspector frequently lost grip and Peter had to wait patiently while the man's numbed fingers fought to take a fresh hold.

Peter let out a long, relieved breath. The worm of unwound tape was getting longer and longer and then, quite suddenly, he was able to move his wrists against each other and jerk his hands free.

'Oh! Well done!' Peter gasped as the Inspector's hands fell away. The effort had clearly exhausted him.

Ray had put the roll of tape and the knife back into the top drawer of the cabinet. Now that Peter's hands were free, it took him only a few moments to pull himself and the chair over to the cabinet. He took the knife out and began to saw away at the tape that held him to the chair.

Inspector Truelove was mumbling to himself again. It sounded as if he was saying, 'Get help, must get help,' over and over again.

Peter sliced his way through the tape.

'I will!' he panted. 'Just as soon as I can get this stuff off me!'

Peter cut through the last few centimetres of tape that held his ankles. He sprang over to the bed. The Inspector's chain was held by a padlock. There was no way of getting him free without a key.

'I'll have to leave you,' said Peter. 'I'll phone the police.' The man's eyes had closed. Peter shook him. 'Inspector? Oh, heck!'

Inspector Truelove had lapsed into unconsciousness.

Peter spun round. He heard a noise on the stairs. Someone was coming back up to the room.

'Right!' Peter said grimly to himself. 'We'll see about this!' He picked up the chair and stood behind the door. He took a firm grip and lifted the chair above his head.

It wasn't in Peter's nature to be violent, but desperate situations called for desperate action. The next person to so much as show a head through that doorway was going to get a big surprise!

*    *    *

'I knew we shouldn't have left him!' said Miranda as she stared at the empty chair in the empty room where they had last seen Peter.

'We didn't have any choice, if you remember,' said Holly. 'If we'd stayed, they'd have caught all of us. At least we're free.' She gave Miranda a determined look. 'One of us should go for help while the other one keeps an eye on things here.'

Miranda thought for a moment then nodded.

'Ok,' said Holly. 'I'll stay. You go.'

Miranda shook her head. 'You go,' she said. 'You can run faster than me.'

'But I'm better at keeping hidden than you are,' said Holly. 'You'd probably bump into something, or sneeze or fall over. You know what you're like.'

'I can stay as well-hidden as you can,' said Miranda. 'I'm staying, and that's that.'

Holly looked at her. 'It was my idea to come here in the first place,' she said coaxingly. 'It's my fault! I think you should go and I should stay.'

Miranda frowned. 'OK,' she said reluctantly.

'But I don't like leaving you here. It feels like I'm running away.'

'I'll keep out of trouble,' said Holly. 'Don't worry.'

Miranda looked at her. 'It'll be the first time ever if you do,' she said. 'But promise you'll be careful.'

'I will,' said Holly.

The decision made, they headed for the window through which they had entered the building.

'Go due south,' Holly instructed Miranda. 'You've got the compass. You know how to use it, don't you?'

'Of course I do,' said Miranda. She gripped her friend's arm. 'Shh!'

They could hear voices approaching. The two girls slipped into an alcove and pressed themselves against the wall as the sound of voices came closer along the hallway.

'It was a waste of time, searching in this fog,' said one man. 'Ray's getting jumpy, if you ask me.'

'He's just doing his job,' said a second man. 'You'd expect him to be wired up this close to Zero Hour.'

'I still say those kids were never here,' said the first man. 'The boy was on his own. We should just cut his throat and have done with it.'

An icy shiver went through Holly as she heard this.

A distant shout sounded.

'We're here!' called the first man.

There was the clamour of running feet.

'What is it?' shouted the first man. 'What's happened?'

A third voice spoke urgently. Ray's voice.

'The Prime Minister is crossing the moor this evening,' he said breathlessly. 'He could be here in less than two hours. I just got it out of Truelove. We've got to move fast.'

'What about the boy?' asked the second man.

'I've dealt with him,' said Ray. 'He's up with Truelove. We can forget about them. Come on, we don't have much time.'

The three men ran off, leaving Holly and Miranda staring at each other.

'Did you hear what he said?' breathed Miranda. 'The Prime Minister!'

'That's what all this is about!' said Holly. 'They're going to kidnap the Prime Minister.'

Miranda grabbed Holly's wrist. 'Come with me,' she said, pulling Holly out into the hallway.

'What? Where?'

'Their boss said Peter is with Inspector True-love,' said Miranda. 'We can rescue him now. Which way to that part of the house, though? Can you work it out?'

'I think so,' said Holly.

The two girls ran back towards the empty restaurant room. The two-storey part of Dreath House lay to the right of there. They ran through the large room and into deserted kitchens at the back. A door led them to a corridor. The corridor took a sharp turn and they found themselves at the foot of a flight of stairs.

They exchanged a quick glance of triumph before Holly leaped up the stairs with Miranda only a hair's-breadth behind her.

There were only two doors on the upper corridor. Holly opened the first one. The room was empty.

'This has got to be it!' said Miranda. She

turned the handle on the second door and pushed it open.

She gave a yell of shock as something large and dark came swinging through the air towards her head.

# 10 Escape from Dreath House

'Miranda!' Peter yelled as he realised who it was that had opened the bedroom door.

*'Yowp!'* Miranda shrieked, just ducking in time as the edge of the chair went whistling past her ear. 'Peter! For heaven's sake!'

The chair crashed to the floorboards. There hadn't been time for him to pull back from the downward swing.

Holly was taken by surprise as Miranda suddenly stopped dead in front of her. She toppled over Miranda's bent back and the two of them went sprawling on the floor.

The three friends winced as the noise echoed through the building. Miranda sat up, rubbing where she had bumped her forehead on the floor as Holly had fallen over her.

Peter kicked the chair aside and pulled the two girls to their feet.

'I know what this is all about!' he said urgently. 'They—'

'They're going to kidnap the Prime Minister!' interrupted Miranda.

Peter stared at her with his mouth open. 'I know,' he said. 'How did you find out?'

'We overheard them talking about it,' said Holly. She glanced over Peter's shoulder. 'Inspector Truelove!' she said. 'He isn't . . . I mean . . . they haven't . . .'

'It's OK,' said Peter. 'He's not dead. He's just passed out. They've pumped him full of the truth drug. Ray's just been up here. The Prime Minister is going to be crossing the moor in a couple of hours.'

'We've got to get out of here!' said Miranda.

Holly looked at the Inspector. 'We can't just leave him.'

'We've got to,' said Peter. 'There's no way of getting him loose.'

Holly could see that Peter was right.

Miranda ran to the door and listened.

'I hear something,' she said. 'They're bound to have heard all that racket we made. I think they're heading this way.'

'Quick,' said Holly. 'Lock the door.'

'Lock it with what?' asked Miranda. 'There's no key.'

'Can we drag the bed over in front of it?' suggested Peter. 'That should slow them down a bit.'

'Long enough for us to get out through there!' Holly said, pointing towards the window.

Miranda slammed the door shut and the three of them dragged the heavy old iron bed across the floor. Inspector Truelove moved restlessly on the mattress and mumbled to himself as they brought the bedstead scraping over the bare boards.

'Now!' said Holly. 'One good shove!'

Metal legs screeched on wooden boards as they used all their strength to send the bedstead thumping up against the closed door.

Holly ran to the window.

'Help me,' she called. Three pairs of hands hammered up under the cross-bar of the lower sash and the window grated open. Wisps of fog and cold air came fingering into the room.

There was a loud bang as someone tried to get the bedroom door open and found it blocked.

Holly leaned through the window. She couldn't see the ground for the fog.

'There's something blocking the door!' a voice shouted from outside the room.

'Out of the way!' said another voice. 'I'll get it open!'

Holly straddled the windowsill. There was no time to think about the drop. She drew her other leg out, then turned and slowly lowered herself down the outside wall until her arms were at full stretch and she was clinging on by her fingers.

Two anxious faces peered down at her as she gathered her courage and let go. Cold air swirled round her as she fell. But she landed well, bending her knees to absorb the impact.

Peter followed her out through the window.

A screeching noise made Miranda's head snap round. The bedstead was being pushed back by the men on the other side of the door. There was already a gap wide enough for an arm to force its way through and for a hand to grope into the room.

Peter jumped and Miranda scrambled after him. She got a good grip on the sill with both hands and wormed herself round. As she lowered herself she saw the bedstead lurch forwards. A burly shoulder forced itself through the widening gap.

Miranda let go.

She landed with a force that jarred right up through her body, and found herself in the supporting hands of her two friends.

'Run!' said Holly.

They followed her into the thick blanket of fog. They heard a shout from above them, but already the tall dark side of the house had vanished in the fog.

A single crack rang out.

'That was a gun!' gasped Peter. 'They're shooting at us.'

'They can't see us,' said Miranda. 'We'll be OK. I think.'

The low wall loomed in front of Holly. She vaulted over it and ran across the road. The hillock behind which they had hidden earlier swam into sight.

'This way,' she called, the air raw in her throat.

The three phantom shapes of the friends circled the hill. Holly took a moment to grab their rucksack from where they had left it. She pulled it on.

'Miranda, get the compass,' she said. 'We need to go south.'

Miranda stuck her hand into her back jeans pocket and pulled the compass out.

'Oh, no!' she groaned.

'What?' asked Peter. 'Don't you know how to use it?'

'No one could use *this*!' she said, holding the compass out on her open palm. The glass face was smashed and the little rod on which the needle should have been sitting was bent flat.

'Oh, Miranda!' said Holly, staring at the useless compass.

'It must have happened when I landed on that car,' said Miranda. 'No wonder my behind hurts!'

'OK,' said Holly. 'Let's not panic.' She pointed away into the fog. 'We know the campsite is that way. All we've got to do is to try to keep going straight.' She looked at them. 'I mean, how hard can it be to walk in a straight line?'

'Harder than you'd think,' said Peter. 'I was

watching a programme on telly the other week. It was about people who get lost in deserts. Apparently they wander round and round in circles until their water runs out.'

'And then they get eaten by vultures, I suppose,' said Miranda. 'Thanks for sharing that with us, Peter.'

'The point is that they think they're going in a straight line, but they're not,' Peter explained patiently. 'It's something to do with the fact that you take longer strides with one leg than you do with the other, which automatically sends you around in circles.'

'Are you sure about that?' asked Holly.

Peter nodded. 'If you're right-handed, it means you'll automatically veer to the right,' he said. 'So what you do is to take a slight turn to the left every one hundred steps. That's what it said in the programme.'

'You watch the weirdest programmes,' said Miranda. 'Your TV must be tuned into some bizarre channels.'

'I really think we'd better get moving,' said Holly. There was no actual sound of pursuit from the house, but Holly hadn't forgotten the sound of that single gunshot. And she was in no doubt that Ray would send his men out after them.

She wanted to put as much distance as possible between them and the armed terrorists as quickly as they could.

They plunged into the fog, trotting along together while Peter counted.

'One hundred!' he said.

Holly turned left.

'That's too much, I think,' Peter told her.

Holly altered course again so they were heading slightly to the left of what seemed the straight way ahead.

'This is crazy,' muttered Miranda as Peter started counting again. 'We really will end up going in circles if we keep this up. We'll end up right back at Dreath House!'

They trotted on through the fog, jinking left every one hundred paces. Miranda was growing more and more certain that Peter's crazy idea was sending them in one big loop right back to where they had started.

'The road!' panted Holly. The valley had appeared suddenly right in front of them, filled with dense fog, like a river full of murky water.

'At least that means we're more or less on course,' said Holly as they scrambled down the valley side. 'If only a car would come along!'

They stepped out on to the tarmac. Holly paused, her eyes baffled by the thick fog. She strained her ears for the sound of a car. But the moor was silent. The only sound was the rasp of their own breath.

'We're wasting our time,' said Peter. 'I don't think this road is used much. That's probably why the Prime Minister decided to come this way. He probably thought it was safer than the motorway.'

'If we don't get some help pretty soon,' Miranda said grimly, 'he's going to find out how wrong he is!'

'Don't even think about that,' said Holly. 'We'll get help!'

She ran to the far side of the road and clawed her way up the steep hillside. If they kept up this pace, and if Peter was right about how to keep in a straight line, then they should be at the campsite in half an hour or less.

Then all they had to do was phone the police.

The fact that they knew the route and timing of the Prime Minister's journey should be enough to convince anyone they spoke to that they were telling the truth.

They trotted on through the rough, hummocky terrain.

Peter came to a sudden halt, spreading his arms out.

'Shh!' he said.

'What?' Miranda panted.

'I thought I heard something,' said Peter. 'Listen!'

'What did you hear?' asked Holly. 'I can't hear a thing.'

Peter frowned. 'I thought I heard a voice.' He pointed to the right. 'Over there. I'm sure I did.'

'Maybe it'll be someone who can help us,' said Miranda.

'Or maybe it's one of *them*,' Holly said ominously. She shook her head. 'We can't risk it. We'll go the other way.'

The renewed fear of pursuit set all their nerves on edge. And in the thick fog it was possible to imagine that armed men were stalking them only a few metres away. At any moment a dreaded shadow could loom up and they'd be done for.

Holly gave a cry of alarm and lurched backwards as a dark shape appeared through the fog. It was a man. A man crouching as though ready to pounce. And Holly was certain that she saw the dark shadow of a gun in his hand.

'Oh!' Holly blinked as the menacing shape suddenly melted into the ragged grey outlines of one of the Dragon Stones. The gun was just a lump of lichen.

'You big twit!' said Miranda. 'You almost scared me to death.' She stepped forwards and gave the standing stone a pat. 'Come on,' she said, 'I'll take the lead, seeing that you can't tell the difference between stones and boogie-men.'

Holly felt hot and cold all over with her fright.

'Sorry,' she said. 'My eyes are beginning to play tricks on me.'

'Tell me about it,' said Miranda with a laugh. She narrowed her eyes as she peered into the fog. 'Mind you, I don't blame you,' she said. 'You could easily mistake some of these stones for people. I mean, take that one over there.' She waved over to their left. 'If I didn't know better, I'd swear that . . . oh, my gosh!'

As Miranda stared at the smoky shape on the very margins of sight, she saw it move. It came towards them, and this time there was no mistaking the shape.

It was a man dressed in black, and in his hand was a gun. It was one of the terrorists. The Mystery Kids had been caught!

 **Fog**

'Run!' shrieked Holly.

The three friends had two things in their favour. The man was as surprised at their sudden appearance as they were by his. And there were *three* of them.

Holly was in no doubt that any one of Ray's men was quite capable of shooting them. But not even the most ruthless killer could shoot in three different directions at the same time.

The three friends scattered, running hard and fast; not caring for the moment about where they were going. The only thought in their minds was to get away from the man.

Holly heard a shout and then the horrible crack of gunfire. A loud, ringing whine sounded close to her ear, followed by the pa-kow! of a ricochet as a bullet struck one of the standing stones not half a metre to her left.

She kept on running until her foot caught on a hummock of rough grass. She found herself rolling over and over down a shallow slope. She came to a thudding, sprawling halt, dizzy and winded.

She lay staring up into the fog, panting and gasping for breath.

*Think*, she said to herself. *There was only the one shot. That's good. But what do I do now? Look for Miranda and Peter or make for the campsite?*

And then the truth of her situation hit her with a rush. She had no idea which direction she had run in.

She stood up and stared into the blank whiteness. Was she facing south? Or north? Or *what*? She didn't have the faintest idea.

She listened with all her concentration. There wasn't a sound, apart from her own gasps for breath.

She looked round, trying to guess which way to go. If all else failed, intuition would have to serve. She chose a direction, squared her shoulders, and trotted into the fog.

Miranda crouched behind one of the Dragon Stones, trying to breathe quietly although her chest was heaving from her flight from the terrorist.

She had run like mad until a stitch in her side had forced her to seek cover. As she leaned against the cold stone, she pressed a hand into her side, wincing as every indrawn breath seemed to twist the needle of pain under her ribs.

The stone was large: a rugged two metres square, but only thirty-or-so centimetres thick, like a large, rough-hewn paving stone, thrust into the ground.

As her breathing came under control she became aware of a sound, a soft, rhythmic noise which seemed to be coming from the other side of the stone.

It was the sound of laboured breathing. Miranda's heart jumped into her throat. Was it the gunman?

Miranda's whole body stiffened. She heard the soft swish of movement and some puzzling, gutteral, spluttering sounds. It had to be the man.

Miranda was held in an agony of indecision. Should she make a break for it and hope to outrun him? Or should she sit tight and pray for him to wander off?

The swishing sounds moved along the back of the stone. The man was walking to the edge. Another few steps and he would come round to Miranda's side.

Miranda stood up and prepared to fight for her life.

A black wedge-shape appeared round the stone at about knee-height. The wedge-shape turned and a pair of curious eyes gazed at Miranda as a grubby off-white body came into view.

'A *sheep*!' she gasped, almost collapsing into the grass in her relief. The animal stared at her, decided it didn't like the look of her, and trotted off into the fog.

Miranda grinned. She'd been frightened by a sheep. A stupid, harmless sheep!

A hand came down on her shoulder and she let out a piercing shriek.

Holly was uncertain. She had come into an area strewn with small stones. She didn't remember seeing anything like this before – certainly not on the way to or from the campsite.

*I think I'm going west*, she said to herself. *I think that's what's happened*

West was no good. Holly knew she would have to walk for several kilometres to the west before she got anywhere.

She did an about-face and headed back the way she had come. She longed for some recognisable feature to appear through the fog. The slope that led to the road. The three rings of standing stones. Anything to give her some hint of where she was.

But more than anything else, she longed for the familiar shapes of Peter and Miranda to come walking out of the endless whiteness.

She halted in her tracks as a brief wail sounded through the air. It cut off suddenly and the silence of the moor closed in once again. But Holly recognised the voice. It was Miranda!

Holly ran in the direction from which the cry had sounded. If Miranda was in trouble, then she was going to help.

The grim shapes of the Dragon Stones loomed round Holly as she ran. She was almost back to the place where they had first encountered the armed man.

And then she saw two shapes – two human shapes crouching in the lee of one of the stones.

'Holly!' gasped Miranda. 'Thank heavens!'

Holly could have hugged them. Miranda and Peter were huddled together against the stone.

Holly came crashing down on to her knees.

'You screamed,' she panted. 'Why did you scream?'

'Because Peter came up behind me and scared me silly!' said Miranda.

'I was trying to keep *quiet*,' explained Peter. 'And then she goes and yells like a banshee.' He looked at Holly. 'If you heard her, *he* must have done as well.'

'We'd better move,' said Holly.

They got up.

'Which way?' asked Miranda. 'Has anyone got any ideas?'

'Not back there,' said Holly, hooking a thumb over her shoulder. 'I've been that way. It's all wrong.'

A curious crackling noise drifted on the swirling air.

'What was that?' whispered Miranda.

'A walkie-talkie,' Peter whispered back. 'Shh!'

They listened as the crackling noise continued

for a few more seconds. Then they heard the muffled voice of one of the men. Not right on top of them, but far too close for comfort.

Holly put her finger to her lips and beckoned for her two friends to follow her.

They slipped away into the fog in the opposite direction from which the voice had come.

'I don't think they're going to give up,' whispered Peter. 'They're going to keep searching until they find us.'

'Then we'll have to keep hidden,' said Holly. She looked at her watch. It was half past five.

She was about to speak again when Miranda pulled her and Peter down. Silently Miranda pointed. A faint, hazy grey shape was moving on the very edge of sight. Moving quickly and purposefully.

The crackle of a walkie-talkie sounded again. The ghostly shape melted into the fog.

'They're all around us,' murmured Peter. 'I think they're closing in.'

'They don't know where we are,' whispered Holly. 'Come on, let's keep moving.'

They kept low, creeping over the rugged

terrain of the moor with eyes and ears straining. Several minutes went by without any sight or sound of the men.

'Do you think we've lost them?' whispered Miranda.

'I hope so,' said Holly. She straightened up to ease her aching back. 'Is that what I think it is?' she said, pointing into the opaque distance.

Peter and Miranda followed the line of her finger. A large grey shape humped itself up through the fog.

'That must be Butterwrench Tor,' said Peter. 'Hey! If we climb up to the top we might be able to see where we are. It might be above the fog.'

'That's exactly what I was thinking,' said Holly with renewed hope. 'Come on.'

The rocky hill was further away than they had imagined. As they approached it, the shape darkened and became more solid, rearing up like the back of some gigantic sleeping animal.

They began to climb.

Holly noticed that the fog thinned as they clambered upwards. Up on the long back of the Tor the mist blew in wavering banners and the sky was a milky blue. Away over to their left the sun burned in the western sky.

All round them was a sea of grey, but in one direction they could see the dark green of trees.

'That's the way back!' said Holly. 'That's where the campsite is.'

'OK,' said Miranda. 'Let's go!'

'Be careful,' Holly warned as her friend began to scramble down the side of the hill. Miranda vanished into the blanket of fog.

Holly called after her. 'Remember what happened last time you – Miranda!'

A stone moved unexpectedly under Miranda's foot and she fell. But she didn't fall far. A figure appeared through the fog, seemingly out of nowhere. She saw eyes widen. She saw a mouth open to speak and a hand rise with a gun in it.

And then she crashed into the man. He let out a gasp as he over-balanced. The gun wheeled out of his grasp.

The world seemed to turn somersaults as Miranda and the man went tumbling head over heels down the steep hillside.

 **Zero hour**

Miranda felt as if she was in a tumble-drier as she rolled over and over down the hillside. When she finally came to a jarring halt, it was against something soft. Her brain was whirling round like a top, but at least she wasn't hurt.

There was a low groan. The something she had landed on shifted for a moment then became still.

She sat up. It was the Rat. He was sprawling on the ground like a discarded rag-doll. Miranda scrambled away from him, her eyes narrowed, limbs ready for flight.

But the man didn't move. Miranda crept nearer again and gave him a shove. There was no reaction. The man was unconscious.

Miranda stood up. She felt woozy.

'That'll teach you to mess with us!' she said. A noise from above her made her look round.

Holly and Peter slid into view through the fog, their faces twisted with anxiety.

Miranda grinned at them. 'I got him!' she said.

'Are you sure he's out?' said Peter. 'Where's his gun?'

'He's out, all right,' said Miranda. A brief search failed to come up with the gun. It must have bounced clear as they fell and lost itself in some crevice.

An electronic crackling noise brought their eyes back to the spreadeagled terrorist. It was his walkie-talkie. But this time they were close enough to be able to understand the voice that squawked through it.

'Captain to all units,' said Ray's distorted voice. 'Call off the search. Repeat: call off the search. I have returned to base and picked up the car. Meet me on the road.'

The crackle ceased.

Miranda gave a low whistle. 'They're giving up,' she said. 'We've made it!'

'But you realise why, don't you?' said Holly. 'It's six o'clock.'

'We're not going to have time to get all the way to the campsite,' said Peter. 'By the time we get on to the police, the Prime Minister will already be here.'

'So, what are we waiting for?' said Miranda. 'We've got to stop the Prime Minister's car before they do. We've got to warn him.'

Peter nodded. 'Back to the road then,' he said.

This time the three friends didn't waste a moment talking about it. Holly still had a fairly clear idea of the direction in which they should go.

They trotted through the billowing clouds of fog. The wind had strengthened over the last few minutes, and already they found themselves able to see a little further than before.

Holly saw the dark ridge of the valley-side that ran down to the road. She stopped, gesturing to the others to do likewise.

Cautiously they crept to the edge. The fog writhed in the steep valley, driven by the rising wind. Every now and then a gust would tear through the fog so that a clear stretch of the road could be seen.

The road was deserted.

'If I've got it right,' said Holly, 'we're

east of where we saw them rehearsing the kidnapping.'

Peter pointed to their right. 'The Prime Minister will be coming from that direction,' he said. 'So all we need to do is flag the car down as it comes past.'

'Listen!' hissed Miranda.

It was the low growl of an approaching car – coming from the right.

'That could be it!' said Holly. 'Quick.'

She and Miranda began to scramble down the hillside, but for some reason Peter hesitated. He stood up on the edge of the slope and peered into the fog.

He let out a gasp. A sudden squall of wind swept the curtain of fog aside for a few moments, allowing him to see a long stretch of roadway.

'Holly! Miranda!' shouted Peter. 'Get back. It's *them*!'

Through the swirls of fog he had clearly seen the red car used by the kidnappers.

The two girls hurled themselves back up the slope and all three of them flattened themselves into the ground as the familiar car approached.

They heard it pass beneath them and then slow down. Holly wriggled around and wormed her way closer to the edge. The red car had come to a halt at the roadside.

As she watched from cover, Ray and his two remaining men got out. They were too far away for her to be able to hear them talking, but the fog had thinned enough for her to see everything that they did.

She could see that Ray was giving orders. The car was steered off the road. Holly noticed that there was a dip at the roadside, like a wide ditch. The men pushed the car so that its front wheels bumped down into the ditch. It looked exactly as if it had driven off the road and crashed.

Anyone stopping to offer assistance would not realise the car was undamaged until it was too late. But the kidnappers hadn't finished. One of them sat in the driver's seat. Holly saw Ray take something out of his pocket. A jar or a tube of some sort. He held it up to the man in the car and Holly saw red liquid pour out.

It was fake blood. Ray was making absolutely certain that the next car to come along that road would have to stop and help. No one would drive straight past an injured man.

Holly edged backwards.

'We'll have to get further away,' she said, pointing to the right. 'We mustn't let them see us.'

They pulled back from the edge and ran at a crouch until Holly was certain that they were out of sight of the three men.

'What if the Prime Minister's car won't stop for us?' asked Peter.

'We'll have to make sure it does!' said Miranda.

'Yes,' said Peter. 'But—'

He was interrupted by a strangulated howl from Holly and the fierce grip of her fingers on his arm. She was staring along the road.

'I can hear a car!' she gasped.

'Oh, heck!' exclaimed Miranda. She didn't pause to think. She jumped over the edge of the slope. Somehow she managed to keep to her feet as she went skidding and skittering down the steep fall in an explosion of stones and dust.

Holly and Peter were taken by surprise by Miranda's madcap leap, but they were quick to follow her.

It was impossible for Miranda to control the speed of her descent. All she could do was to keep upright and hope for the best. She hit the roadside and staggered forwards into the middle of the road, her arms windmilling as she tried to save herself from crashing on to her face on the tarmac.

She saw the car approaching at speed. A large, dark grey car. Dizzily, she planted herself in the middle of the road and stretched her arms up.

She had the briefest possible impression of a startled face through the windscreen. There was the gleam of on-rushing metal and the powerful roar of the engine.

For a split second Miranda thought they were going to drive straight over her.

But then the air was rent by the fearsome screech of rubber on tarmac as the driver braked furiously. The back end of the car slewed round. Miranda closed her eyes, expecting to be hit.

The terrible scream of brakes stopped. Miranda opened her eyes. The car had swung to a halt, its side about ten centimetres away from her. She blinked at a shocked face through a side window.

Three of the doors burst open. Two men and a women leaped out of the car.

'You stupid fool,' shouted one of the men. 'You could have been killed!'

'Kidnappers!' Miranda screamed at the top of her voice, gesticulating wildly along the road. 'Waiting for you! Down there!'

At that moment, Holly and Peter caught up with their friend.

'It's true,' gasped Holly. 'They're pretending they've had an accident. They're going to kidnap the Prime Minister.'

The window of the fourth door wound down with a soft electronic whirr and a face stared out at them. A face all three of them recognised. They'd seen it in newspapers and on the television. It was the Prime Minister.

'They kidnapped Inspector Truelove,' said Peter. 'They're holding him in a big old house. They gave him a truth drug so he'd tell them what time you'd be here.'

One of the men pulled a slim mobile phone out of his jacket pocket and punched out a number.

Seconds later he was speaking rapidly into

the phone, giving orders for reinforcements for the capture of the kidnappers.

The three friends looked at one another, their eyes gleaming with relief. They'd done it!

Holly and the others explained everything during the tense wait for more help to arrive. Only a few minutes later two more cars drove up at speed, filled with armed security officers.

There was a brief discussion before the two cars and all but one of the security officers headed into the rapidly thinning mist.

The three friends waited silently.

They heard gunshots and shouts. It sounded like the terrorists were putting up a fight.

'Get into the car,' said the security man who had stayed with the Prime Minister. 'It'll be safer.'

The Prime Minister opened the door and the three friends crammed into the back. They stared through the windows, their hearts in their mouths.

Abruptly the shooting stopped.

'That sounds like the end of it,' said the security guard. 'I'll just go and check.'

He opened the door and stepped out. There

was a sudden rush of noise and a blur of movement. Holly saw the figure of the terrorist leader came jumping down the hillside, a ferocious grimace twisting his face.

'Keep down!' shouted the Prime Minister. He threw himself protectively over the three friends.

The car shook as the security guard was driven back by the force of Ray's attack. Miranda found herself tangled up on the narrow floor space in the back of the car with the Prime Minister's arm across her. Her heel hit a button on the door and the window automatically wound itself down.

A desperate fight was going on outside the rocking car. Holly could see that Ray had lost his gun and that there was blood on the sleeve of one arm. He was gripping the security guard's wrist with both hands, trying to wrench the gun out of his fingers.

As they fought, Ray's elbow came thrusting into the car. Holly threw herself forwards, across the Prime Minister, and jammed the heel of her hand against the automatic window button to close the window again. The sheet of glass slid upwards.

Ray gave a yell as his arm was trapped. The next second he let out a low gasp and his body slumped sideways. Holly saw what happened. A skilled blow with the edge of the security guard's hand had taken all the fight out of the terrorist leader.

The face of the triumphant security guard peered in through the window.

'Is everyone OK in there?' he asked.

'I think so,' said the Prime Minister.

'We're all fine,' said Holly.

Seconds later the two cars drove back down the road and came to a halt. The rest of the Prime Minister's guards came running over. Ray was carried to one of the cars and put in the back, where the other two terrorists were already being held. No one had been hurt in the brief gunfight, except for Ray, who had been shot in the arm before escaping up the hillside.

The man in charge of the security force took the three friends to one side.

'I know who those men are,' he told them. 'Their leader's name is Raymond Mazerra. They belong to a terrorist group that calls itself the Black Flag.'

Holly and her friends gazed at him in amazement.

'If his mission had succeeded,' the man continued, 'which it would have done without your help, the Prime Minister would have been in terrible danger.' He smiled. 'You should feel very proud of yourselves!'

Miranda looked at him with circular eyes.

'I hope you don't think I'm being pushy or anything,' she said, 'but is there any chance of us getting a *medal* for this?'

'Good grief,' said Holly, not for the first time. 'That was so embarrassing! Fancy asking for a medal!'

'Well, why not?' Miranda said coolly. 'Don't we deserve one? Did we or did we not save the Prime Minister from being kidnapped? If that's not worth a medal or two, I'd like to know what is.'

'That's all very well,' said Holly. 'But you're not supposed to ask for one.'

'Aw, pooh!' said Miranda. 'Don't ask: don't get, my grannie always says.' She leaned over the front passenger seat of the car, her arm resting on Peter's shoulder. 'What do you think, Mr Hamilton? Shouldn't we get a medal or something?'

Peter's father laughed. 'We'll see,' he said.

It was the following morning and they were driving to the official opening of the Royal West Country Show.

'I don't really mind if we don't get a medal,' Miranda said as she sat back down next to Holly in the back of the car. 'But I will ask for an autograph.' She looked across at Holly. 'Unless that's too embarrassing for you to cope with.'

Holly smiled. 'No, I think I can handle that,' she said.

'Here we are!' said Peter. They had just come over the crest of a hill. The huge site of the show spread out before them. There was a vast carpark already half-filled with cars. Men in yellow coats were directing the traffic. And the show itself seemed to go on for ever. There were tents and marquees and stalls and fascinating-looking constructions as far as the eye could see.

An airship cruised overhead and music poured from loudspeakers.

'Do you think we could get a ride in the

airship?' asked Miranda, craning her neck to see the fat silver shape as it glided through the cloudless sky. 'I've always fancied that.'

'Maybe,' said Mr Hamilton. 'If you have time between all the other things you've got to do today.'

'Sorry?' asked Holly. 'What things?'

Mr Hamilton grinned. 'Oh, didn't I tell you? I got a call late last night. You're to attend a press conference this morning. To tell everyone exactly what happened yesterday. And then you're being taken out to lunch by the Prime Minister.' He laughed at the astonished expression on the faces of the three friends. 'It must have slipped my mind.'

'Oh, wow!' breathed Miranda as Mr Hamilton drove the car straight past the queue for the ordinary carpark and in through an entrance which was signposted: 'VIPs only'. 'Oh, wow, oh, wow, oh, wow!'

The Mystery Kids looked at one another, their faces split by enormous grins. A press conference! Lunch with the Prime Minister! There really was only one thing to say to all that, and Miranda was already saying it.

'Oh, wow!'